A MOST ELIGIBLE BACHELOR

BY

JESSICA STEELE

*First published in Great Britain 1998
Large Print edition 1999
Harlequin Mills & Boon Limited,
Eton House, 18-24 Paradise Road,
Richmond, Surrey TW9 1SR*

© Jessica Steele 1998

ISBN 0 263 15938 8

*Set in Times Roman 16½-18
16-9903-51420 C*

*Printed and bound in Great Britain
by Antony Rowe Ltd, Chippenham, Wiltshire*

CHAPTER ONE

JAZZLYN knew that she would never marry. It didn't worry her; she seldom thought about it. It was just there, rock-solid in her head.

It was not that she disliked men. As was normal for any unattached twenty-two year old, she went out on dates—although as soon as she saw the merest flicker that the man in question was starting to be remotely serious she took evasive action. She didn't go out with the man again. Three dates with the same man was usually her limit.

She drove home from her secretarial job with one of London's major law firms that Wednesday evening, realising that what had put thoughts of marriage, or in her case, never marrying, in her head was the fact that her father seemed to be growing more and more serious about his present lady-friend. And Grace Craddock—unlike, it had to be said, a good few of his previous female 'friends'—*was* a lady.

His other attachments had seldom endured longer than a few months. But it was six months now since Jazzlyn's father had introduced her to the woman he had met at some Christmas party or other. Grace was older than most of the other women her father had brought home. She was around fifty-five, two years younger than Edwin Palmer, and had divorced her philandering husband some years before. Jazzlyn's father had been married three times—but was he thinking of marrying for a fourth time?

Her worry over the prospect, Jazzlyn realised, was the reason why she had marriage on her mind so much. She wanted her father to be happy, of course she did, and Grace too—she had grown very fond of Grace. But was her father cut out for marriage? On the face of it, it didn't appear so. Jazzlyn's mother had died when she was five, and she had grown up knowing two stepmothers and a succession of 'aunts', and a home which in the main had been fraught with hysteria, argument, and accusation; at times it had been so truly awful that her father would send her to stay with her grandparents for a while. It hadn't always been over when she returned. But, as a result of so much strife, Jazzlyn had known from a very early age that if that was marriage, if that was how relationships went, then she wanted none of it.

She enjoyed her job at Brown, Latimer and Brown, and knew she was in the running for considerable promotion at the end of the year when one of the senior secretaries took early retirement. A career, Jazzlyn considered—having had dealings with many painful divorce cases in her work—had much more to offer than the current sixty per cent chance of making a happy marriage, if the national average was anything to go by.

But, happy in her work, happy in her life, Jazzlyn drew up her car on the drive of her village home on the outskirts of Buckinghamshire. She entered her home and was immediately besieged by the world's scruffiest dog. 'Hello, Remmy!' She made a fuss of the mixed breed hound which had ambled into her father's studio about six years ago, lain down at her father's feet, subsequently been invited to share her father's lunch, and had—while free to leave—shown a most decided aversion to doing so. Having adopted them—Jazzlyn had checked everywhere to see if he had been reported missing; he was distinctive by his scruffiness alone— and with no one willing to claim him, it seemed, he had stayed.

Jazzlyn put the kettle on to boil. Her father would have heard her car and, depending upon how deeply involved he was on his present painting, he would come through for a cup of tea soon.

'And I expect you'd like a biscuit?' she addressed Rembrandt, whom she guessed had departed the studio when he'd heard her car.

He was already moving his tail from side to side, but at the mention of the word 'biscuit' began to thump it furiously.

Jazzlyn fed him a dog biscuit and was just warming the teapot at the kitchen sink when she spotted a long, sleek car coming up the drive. 'Expensive,' she murmured, though she wasn't entirely unused to her father having the occasional wealthy client who wanted a portrait painted. Her father could have been wealthy too, had he taken all the portrait work offered. But he didn't enjoy it, preferring to paint what he wanted to paint, and consequently, good paint and canvas being the price they were, they'd missed out on being in the 'wealthy' bracket. Not that it bothered either father or daughter in the smallest way.

Rembrandt started barking a warning before the car had stopped. Watching from the window as the car halted and a dark-haired man, somewhere in his mid-thirties, extracted his long length, Jazzlyn instructed Rembrandt to 'stay'. The man was clad in a dark business suit—probably he'd just come from his office. He'd love it if the dog left an ample supply of his shaggy, wiry coat all over him.

Leaving the kitchen and closing the door after her—the dog wasn't always trustworthy—Jazzlyn went out into the hall and, for no reason she could think of, found that she was checking her appearance in the long hall mirror. Somehow—except for a few dog hairs—she had managed to remain as close to immaculate at the end of her working day as she had at the beginning.

Five feet eight, slender in her mid-blue two-piece, she checked her hair—thick, long, so blonde as to be almost white—skirted to violet

eyes and a complexion that had once been remarked on as stunning—and the doorbell
sounded. She went quickly to answer it—
mustn't keep her father's clients waiting.

She pulled back the door. He was tall, taller
than her by about eight inches. While her heart
did a giddy, absurd little kind of flip, she
smiled a natural kind of smile as, guessing his
business, she waited for him to announce it.

Strangely, however, he didn't do so straight
away, but stared at her, his eyes first taking in
her colouring, her eyes, her sweetly curving
mouth before he requested politely, 'I'd like to
see Mr Palmer?' His voice was warm, charming, and, Jazzlyn felt, certain to send more than
one female into a flutter.

But, given that—well, yes, she had felt a bit
of a tingle in the region of her spine—she was
made of sterner stuff than that. 'My father
won't be too long now. Would you like to
come in and wait?' She smiled.

'Thank you.'

Jazzlyn was leading the way into the sitting
room before it struck her that she must have
had a more tiring day than she'd realised—she

should have first asked him if he had an appointment to see her father.

She intended to rectify that omission the moment they entered the sitting room. But then the telephone in the hall began to ring.

Jazzlyn opened the sitting room door and held it wide. 'If you'd like to have a seat while I answer that,' she suggested pleasantly, and turned about, to go and quieten the ringing instrument.

'Hello?' she questioned lightly on picking up the phone—and felt her spirits drop when she heard the eager tones of Tony Johnstone. She had been out with Tony the previous evening—for the last time. She had thought he had realised from her cool attitude when he'd started to grow amorous that she wouldn't be going out with him again, but she must have been mistaken.

'I thought you'd be home by now!' he declared enthusiastically.

'I've just got in,' she informed him.

'Shall I see you tonight?'

Oh, heck, he hadn't, it seemed, got the message. 'I'm afraid not,' she answered him civilly.

'Tomorrow?'

Oh, hang it! There was nothing for it, she was going to have to be blunt. 'I'm sorry, Tony. I've enjoyed your company, but I won't be going out with you again,' she felt forced to inform him quietly.

A stunned kind of silence followed—to be broken by an almost wailed, *'Jazzlyn!'* She stood firm. She had liked him, otherwise she would never have gone out with him to start with, and she hated to hurt anyone's feelings, but he couldn't be *that* distraught. But apparently he was! 'I thought we had something going?' he persisted after a few moments.

She'd only been out with him four times! 'I'm afraid not,' she replied gently.

'But—but—I was thinking of something long-term!'

This was crazy; they barely knew each other! 'If I gave you that impression, I'm sorry. But...'

'I was hoping, after a few more dates, we might think in terms of us getting engaged!' He refused to take no for an answer.

Engaged! Jazzlyn owned to having a soft heart, and had been hating herself that she was having to be so blunt, but at Tony's suggestion that he was thinking in terms of marriage, something inside her froze. 'There was *never* any question of that, Tony!' she wasted no time in telling him.

'I offended you last night! I came on too strong. I'm sorry,' he apologised hastily. 'I knew I had, but you're so beautiful, so lovely, I just couldn't seem to stop myself. But it won't happen again, I prom—'

This was dreadful! Jazzlyn stopped him right there. 'Tony, listen to me. I have, as I've said, enjoyed your company. But I know that there is no point in our going out together again.'

'But…' he started to protest.

'So, I'd be very pleased if, for me to keep the memory of the good times we had, you didn't ring me again.'

'But I want to *marry you*!'

After four dates! 'Then, Tony, I'm sorry— very sorry—but I do *not* want to marry you!' She felt forced to be even more blunt.

'Jazzlyn!'

'Goodbye, Tony,' she said quietly, and, while feeling all upset and anxious inside, somehow she just couldn't slam the phone down on him, but did him the courtesy of waiting to hear his goodbye before she replaced the receiver.

It came after a very long pause. 'You'll ring me, write to me, get in touch if you change your mind?' he questioned.

'Of course,' she said, knowing that would never happen, but, taking his question as his goodbye, she quietly put down her phone. She was starting to feel a mixture of sadness for having hurt his feelings and a touch of irritation that Tony Johnstone had been thinking along the lines he had, when she turned—and got the shock of her life. Tony Johnstone's astonishing proposal—for that, she saw, was what his talk of marriage amounted to—had taken completely from her mind all memory that her father had a visitor. Though had she given that fact a thought she would have assumed the visitor was safely seated in the sitting room with the door closed, comfortably out of earshot.

But not so. The dark-haired man, having ignored her invitation to go into the sitting room, had budged not an inch from where she had left him! Instead he was standing there—and had been openly listening to every word of her rejection of Tony Johnstone's proposal!

And just to prove that he was not in the slightest deaf—and without the tiniest hint of apology for having been so blatantly tuned in to her conversation—he commented, 'Rough!' He actually had the gall to refer to it.

Jazzlyn began to feel all hot and bothered, and wished she could remember word for word what she had said. 'It—had to be done,' she excused, though she felt more like telling him to mind his own business, but remembered in time that this man was her father's client.

'Had to?' he had the audacity to question.

Jazzlyn had not the smallest intention of continuing this conversation. But oddly she found—maybe it was just something compelling about the visitor, or perhaps her tendency to ever be open and honest—that she was answering. 'My fault—I should have seen it coming, but I must have completely missed the signs.'

'Signs?'

Jazzlyn stared at him. He knew what she meant, but clearly he was a man who liked to know everything. Could he go run! So—why did she find herself answering his question? 'Four dates—and he was talking of waltzing me up the aisle,' she answered. 'I should never have gone out with him that fourth time—I seldom do.'

'Three dates and that's it?'

She couldn't believe she was having this conversation. Nor could she believe she was, again, involuntarily answering. 'Usually—unless it's somebody I've known for ages and who knows I'm not interested in going steady.' At that point Jazzlyn got herself together and was about to politely change the topic—she had already said too much—only it appeared that the stranger hadn't done with it yet.

'You're not interested in marriage?' he asked, quite at ease apparently with what she considered was her conversation.

Her eyes widened, and she was unsure whether to be cross or whether to laugh. 'It's all right for everybody else,' she allowed.

'But not for you?' He was getting in too close; she didn't like it—she didn't know him from Adam, for goodness' sake! She didn't answer. 'Nursing a bruised heart?' he had the colossal nerve to query. And she just had to laugh.

'No way!' she chuckled, her lips parting to reveal her perfect even teeth. She was totally undecided what it was about this man that without effort he could make her laugh when really she felt quite cross. He stared at her and appeared to like what he saw of her sunny expression. But, just as Jazzlyn was wondering what other subject that had nothing to do with him he would ask about, she heard sounds that indicated to her that her father was on his way. 'If you'll excuse me,' she offered politely, aware that he too had picked up the sound of someone coming their way. She met her father at the far end of the hall. 'You've a visitor,' she murmured, and, deciding to take the dog for a walk, went up to her room to change into jeans and a tee shirt.

Jazzlyn and Rembrandt were away from the house for a good hour. And by the time she swung back into the drive she was coming to terms with having hurt Tony Johnstone's feelings. So, all right, she had broken her own rule and gone out with him a fourth time, but she had never given him so much as the smallest hint that she cared in any way deeply for him. And, had he shown that his feelings for her went beyond that of two people just enjoying being out and about, she would have refused to have gone out with him last night.

The expensive-looking car was no longer parked on the drive—she had not expected that it would be. 'Did you have some tea?' she asked her father when she found him leafing through some art magazine in the sitting room—not the first question that sprang to her mind, she had to admit.

That first question was answered by her father, who didn't answer the question she had actually asked, but enquired, 'Did you know who that was?'

'A client?'

Edwin Palmer shook his head. 'Holden Hathaway,' he revealed.

Holden Hathaway? The name sounded familiar. 'Where have I heard that name before?' she asked.

'You'd have heard it if your firm has had any dealings with Zortek International—he's on their board—but...'

'Zortek International?' The name meant nothing to her.

'They're part of some huge conglomerate—something to do with precision engineering, design…' her father replied vaguely, his knowledge seeming only a touch less non-existent than hers, Jazzlyn realised.

'So how do I know his name?' she asked, but even as she asked it bells were starting to ring.

'You must have heard Grace mention him.'

She had. Grace didn't have any children. She did, however, have a nephew. 'He's the nephew Grace thinks so much of,' she remembered. Grace had never mentioned his surname, as far as Jazzlyn could recall, but she had a couple of times mentioned her nephew, Holden, in relation to him doing some task or other for her. 'What was he doing here?' she asked. 'Are you going to paint his portrait?' she went on before he could answer, thinking that perhaps Grace had persuaded her father to undertake the commission.

'Lord, no!' Edwin Palmer scotched any such idea. 'Apart from the fact that I doubt he'd sit still that long, unless he'd got a pile of paperwork in front of him, he's a very busy man, our Mr Hathaway.'

So, if he was so very busy, why had he called to see her father? 'Grace is all right?' Jazzlyn asked quickly; she felt affection for her father's friend and was starting to grow concerned that something might have happened to her.

'Grace is fine,' her father assured her. 'As you know, she's spending a few days with her elder sister, Holden's mother. He looked us up in the phone book, intending to ring, but, seeing our address, he realised he'd be passing this way today and, with his aunt safely in Cornwall, thought he'd call in person.'

Jazzlyn was having a problem with that. 'Why did Grace have to be out of the way?'

'Because it's her birthday a week on Friday, as you know, and he usually takes Grace out for the evening somewhere on her birthday.'

'He's planning a surprise?' Jazzlyn guessed, surmising that for some reason Holden Hathaway felt he had to consult her father about it.

'No—no.' Edwin Palmer hit that notion on the head. 'Grace has apparently spoken to her sister about me, and the way we've seen each other more and more frequently of late, and Holden wondered, that being so, if he'd be treading on my toes, so to speak—if I'd got anything planned for a week on Friday.'

'That was thoughtful of him,' Jazzlyn commented, and meant it. 'Have you?'

'Got anything planned? Well, I had thought of taking Grace to dinner somewhere.'

'You told—er—Holden—this?' Her father nodded. 'What did he say?'

'He at once asked if I'd allow him to host a dinner for the four of us. I said I'd be delighted.' Her father, a thin man of medium height, beamed a smile. 'That okay with you, Jazzlyn.'

'That's fine by me,' she answered cheerfully. 'Which restaurant are you going to, do you know?'

'I said the *four* of us!' her father surprised her by answering. 'You're included.'

'Me!' Jazzlyn got over her surprise to smile at her parent. 'Oh, sorry, I thought when you said four that you meant you and Grace, Holden Hathaway and his wife.'

'He's not married. Never has been. Though from what I can gather, he's not above the odd dalliance or three.' Jazzlyn clearly remembered the man; grey eyes, firm, no-nonsense jaw, and that mouth—humorous, yes, and, well, to be honest, extremely attractive. She could well believe his dalliances went far beyond three. 'You'll come?' her father questioned. 'I'd like you to.'

'I'd love to,' she answered without hesitation. She had no way of knowing if Holden Hathaway had known of her existence before today, and if she had been added to the dinner trio as an afterthought. But, yes, even without her father wanting her there, she was fond enough of Grace to want to be there to celebrate her birthday.

Jazzlyn found she was often thinking of Holden Hathaway in the days that followed. Which in itself she considered to be odd. She was friendly with quite a few members of the opposite sex, but as far as she could recall she was not given to thinking a lot about any of them—save her father, and that was different.

Though thoughts of Holden Hathaway calling as unexpectedly as he had—and why hadn't he told her who he was?—were pushed from her mind on Saturday, when she received a lengthy letter from Tony Johnstone telling her of his love and asking her to phone him.

Feeling that she could not phone him, Jazzlyn penned a letter to him, telling him as gently as she could that she did not love him, and knew that, while she had enjoyed his company and liked him, never *would* she love him.

Then on Monday, she discovered that softening what she'd told him, by telling him she liked him, was the encouragement he'd been looking for. He telephoned her on Monday evening. She had just returned home from work and had barely said hello to Grace, who had arrived that afternoon and was attending to things delicious in the kitchen, when the phone rang.

It was a lengthy phone conversation. At least on Tony's side. But the more he spoke, the more Jazzlyn iced over inside. 'I'm sorry, Tony,' she was forced to tell him in the end, having repeated that she would not go out with him, 'I really must go.' And, snatching at Grace for an excuse, she added, 'We have company I'm neglecting.'

'You look worried,' Grace commented when she joined her, her eyes on her face. 'Anything I can help you with?'

Jazzlyn shook her head, and the sunny side of her nature asserted itself in the face of Grace Craddock's look of concern. 'How did you—tactfully and without hurting any feelings—get rid of *your* unwanted suitors, Grace?' she asked lightly.

'There weren't any. I married Archie Craddock when I was eighteen—rather shutting the door on suitors,' Grace answered, continuing dryly, 'And spent most of the next thirty years learning to regret it.'

'I'm sorry,' Jazzlyn said impulsively.

'Don't be,' Grace smiled. 'All the hurt has long gone. I'm even able to talk to Archie on the phone now without feeling angry.'

'You keep in touch? Do you mind my asking?' Jazzlyn added in a rush.

'Not a bit,' Grace assured her. 'And, yes, we keep in touch. You can't—or at least I can't, no matter how bad Archie's been—cut off thirty blinkered years of trying to make marriage work and walk away as if you'd never known each other. Though it's Archie who rings, not me—usually when he's in some kind of trouble.'

Her father interrupted them by coming in just then. 'How are my two best girls?' he asked, and Jazzlyn saw he was happy.

She took Rembrandt off for a short walk, but again discovered that, though she had thought she might have the worrisome Tony Johnstone on her mind, it was Holden Hathaway who claimed possession. Why it should ferret away at her she didn't know, but he might have introduced himself instead of leaving her to think that he was one of her father's clients.

But why would he introduce himself. If it was her father he'd wanted to see? Yes, but she had been included in that dinner quartet invitation. But then, Holden Hathaway hadn't known before he had met her father what her father's plans, if any, were for Grace's birth-day. That was still no reason for him not to say straight out 'I'm Grace's nephew' Jazzlyn counter-argued to herself—and wondered if she should think of another career; working for a law firm was teaching her to take nothing at face value!

She rescued half a tree trunk from Rembrandt—'No, Remmy—it's too big.'—and headed back for home, striving to dislodge an uncomfortable smidgen of feeling that something was not quite right.

Grace was staying with them for a few days, and Jazzlyn reckoned that she was enjoying Grace's company almost as much as her father was. It was a pleasure to drive home from her place of work in the evening to find Grace—quiet, calm, gentle—just being there, and that was without the delicious meals she cooked!

Jazzlyn pushed thoughts of Holden Hathaway out of her head too. She was not at work now—hang taking nothing at face value! He was a charming, sophisticated man, and most probably in the circles in which he moved he had no need to bother with such trivialities as explaining who he was and what was on his mind to just anybody—albeit she was his aunt's friend's daughter.

Jazzlyn was pleased Grace was staying on another account too. Tony Johnstone had taken to telephoning every night and was becoming a pest. She was glad to have her father's un-ruffled friend to confide in.

'What can I do, Grace?' she asked on Thursday evening, when again Tony phoned.

'Short of taking legal action, which I know you won't, or asking your father to speak to him the next time, which again I know you won't, there's little I can advise, my dear, except that you sit it out. From what you've told me you've given him no encouragement to behave in this fashion. At a guess, I'd say give it a month or so, if you can bear to, and I'm sure by then this young man will have grown tired of getting nowhere and go on to pastures new.'

A month of picking up the phone to find Tony Johnstone on the other end was not a prospect which Jazzlyn looked forward to, but she found that she felt much better for having talked it over with Grace.

Jazzlyn, as seemed always to be the way when she wanted to be home early, was late leaving her office on Friday. Even so, she was home in plenty of time to get ready for the evening.

They were to dine at The Linden, she had discovered. Holden Hathaway must have asked, out of courtesy to her father, where he was thinking of dining, Jazzlyn realised, because The Linden was her father's favourite restaurant. Rex Alford, thirty, divorced, and The Linden's proprietor, was an old friend of Jazzlyn's. She often saw him at parties and had been out with him twice—she had declined his third invitation. They had remained friends, however, and, leaving aside that Rex came from a monied background—his father having bought the restaurant for him—Rex, a businessman to his fingertips, had negotiated commission terms with her father to hang some of his pictures on display in the restaurant.

Holden was calling for them and they were travelling the short distance to the restaurant in his car, apparently. Jazzlyn was in her room when she heard him arrive. She was just about ready and, feeling it impolite to keep their host for the evening waiting, delayed only a sufficient time for him to have greeted his aunt, then left her room.

Grace was looking lovely in a stylish dress of midnight-blue, and Jazzlyn, her white-blonde hair loose about her shoulders and dressed in a sleeveless black dress purchased specially for the occasion, felt that she was looking good too. And, as she met the affable grey eyes of Holden Hathaway, she suddenly experienced a need to want to know she was looking her best.

Her father undertook to introduce her. 'You know my daughter, Jazzlyn.'

'Of course,' Holden replied, and, when strictly speaking he had no need to shake her hand, came forward and stretched out his right hand to her.

His skin was tinglingly warm against her own, and as Jazzlyn murmured a friendly, 'Hello,' and looked up at him, she considered he was just as she remembered him, save that this time, dinner-jacketed, he seemed something else again.

'How are you, Jazzlyn?' he enquired politely.

'Fine,' she replied, and, oddly needing a moment by herself, she added, 'I'll just go and give the hound a guilt-relieving biscuit because we're leaving him all by himself...'

By the time she'd given Rembrandt a few do's and don'ts about his expected behaviour, and switched on the kitchen television for him, everyone was ready to leave.

Somehow, when Grace was the guest of honour, Jazzlyn found that she was the one in the front passenger seat. She turned to comment, but saw that Grace, who was seated in the back and holding hands with Edwin Palmer, seemed more than content.

Her father remarked on what a fine evening it was, and Grace made reference to how lucky she was. Her birthday gifts had been surprising and so very much appreciated.

'You had no idea that Mr Palmer was painting a portrait of you?' Holden enquired.

'None at all! I knew Edwin had done several sketches of me, of course, but the portrait was a total—and very wonderful—surprise.'

Grace sounded thrilled, and Jazzlyn couldn't have been more pleased for her. The portrait had been news to her too—but it showed her the depths of her father's regard for Grace because apart from his now dead first wife, and his daughter, he had never painted the portrait of any female unless there was a fee involved.

Jazzlyn had given Grace a small volume of poetry which she knew Grace especially favoured, and knew that Holden had given his aunt a piece of fine porcelain she had some two months ago expressed an admiration for.

But it was talk of her portrait that held the conversation until they reached The Linden. Jazzlyn did not expect to see the owner. It was a Friday evening, and if she knew Rex Alford he did not employ an excellent staff for nothing. Fridays would mostly find him out somewhere living it up.

But they had barely made it inside the interior when the owner in person came to greet them. Or rather, he came over to greet her. 'Jazzlyn Palmer—I didn't know you had a table reserved for tonight!' he exclaimed.

'I don't tell everybody,' she returned.

He kissed her cheek. 'Still free and running?' he asked, his eyes on her face, clearly enjoying what he saw. 'No man managed to catch you yet?' he asked.

'I'm never without my sprinting shoes,' she laughed.

'You realise you've broken my heart?'

She liked Rex, outrageous flirt that he was. 'I'm sure it will mend,' she replied—and at that moment felt a firm hand on her arm.

Jazzlyn glanced from Rex to the owner of that hand, and saw that Holden was a little impatiently waiting for her to finish her conversation so they could all progress to the small annexe. She didn't know whether to be indignant, surprised or apologetic. But before she could make up her mind she discovered that her father was making introductions and, with a wave generally at a group of pictures on display in the foyer, explaining that they were his.

After that they were soon ensconced at a table in the annexe, with aperitifs before them. Jazzlyn studied the menu that had been placed in her hands by the head waiter but owned to feeling just a touch out of sorts with Holden Hathaway. So, okay, perhaps since he was the host, and since his aunt was the guest of honour, she should have taken a back seat, so to speak. But, hang it all, she'd only been passing a few comments with Rex Alford for a few seconds—thirty at the most, she would swear. So where did Holden Hathaway get off reminding her of her manners? Well, all right, so maybe Rex Alford had seemed as though he'd be perfectly content to stand there chatting solely to her all night, but that was just his way. He didn't mean anything by it—and anyway, what if he did? It was nothing to do with Mr Hoity-toity-mind-your-manners-Hathaway.

Suddenly realising that she was getting all het up and definitely, yes, definitely anti-Holden Hathaway, Jazzlyn pulled herself together. For goodness' sake, this was a dinner for Grace—nothing must be allowed to spoil it. Certainly not Jazzlyn giving their host the cold shoulder.

She looked up from the menu—to find she was staring straight into the steady, unwavering, grey-eyed gaze of the man she had just been mutinying against. His look was cool, impersonal—and clearly he couldn't give a tuppeny damn about what sort of shoulder she gave him, arctic or otherwise. With something of a jolt, Jazzlyn realised no other man of her acquaintance—though Holden remained perfectly polite—was so totally indifferent to her.

'Have you chosen?' he enquired courteously. She was sure she didn't care a button that, after having shown himself to have charm, he was now polite but no more. 'The crab looks interesting,' she returned with pretty politeness, having taken in not a word of what was on offer but certain most restaurants had fish on the menu on Fridays.

After that, Holden Hathaway turned his attention to his aunt, and because of his aunt, and Jazzlyn's affection for her, Jazzlyn pushed any more mutinous thoughts and ponderings on Holden to the back of her mind. Shortly afterwards they adjourned to the table reserved for them. Jazzlyn discovered that before they were halfway through the first course she had forgotten the trace of enmity that had surfaced in her against Holden and that she was able to behave naturally.

Whether or not he was putting himself out to be charming on this special occasion of his aunt's birthday, she had no idea, but by the time they were halfway through their second course Jazzlyn realised that not only was she enjoying herself, but she had so far forgotten the feelings of indignation that Holden had previously aroused that she was also actually enjoying his company.

She even found she liked his sense of humour, and found herself laughing at some small anecdote he recounted. Then she discovered, as she glanced at him, that his grey eyes were on her again, this time warmer than they had been as he took in her laughing mouth and merry eyes.

He looked away abruptly. And she was glad. She had never suffered from a fluttery heartbeat before—but flutter her heart did. She would have to watch that!

A moment later and Jazzlyn was discounting that her heart had fluttered in the slightest. By the time they had finished pudding and were drinking coffee she was certain that, if her heart had fluttered, it was because the fish sauce had been too spiced.

'Oh, by the way.' Edwin Palmer suddenly remembered something, and, addressing his daughter, announced, 'I forgot to tell you. There was a phone call for you just before you got home.' Jazzlyn had an idea who the caller might be and her heart sank. 'A Tony something-or-other,' he recalled, and Jazzlyn was aware of three people looking at her. Grace, who knew all about Tony Johnstone, her father, who didn't, and Holden Hathaway, who had been there when she had asked Tony not to ring her again. 'He said he'd ring again, but I said we were going out and that you'd probably ring him.'

'Thanks Dad,' she said quietly, knowing with certainty she wouldn't.

Somehow she couldn't resist a glance to Holden. He was looking her way, but from his detached expression the whole subject of Tony was of complete uninterest to him. Quite obviously the fact that he'd overheard her tell some man named Tony that she did not wish to marry him was worthy of so little note that Holden had put it so far out of his head as to have forgotten it entirely.

The fact, however, that Holden Hathaway was a man who forgot very little was borne out barely ten minutes later when, the bill settled, they made their way out of the restaurant. At least Jazzlyn and Holden did. The four of them had been making for the exit when, Holden already holding the door open for his aunt to go through, Grace had spotted a picture of Edwin Palmer's which she hadn't seen before. At the same time Jazzlyn espied Rex Alford heading their way.

She'd had too pleasant an evening to want it to end on a sour note, should she be silently accused of forgetting her manners a second time, so, as Grace took it into her head to wander off to inspect the painting, Jazzlyn took it into her head to get out of there.

'Night, Rex, lovely meal,' she called—he was so close, she felt she couldn't very well ignore him—and went quickly through the door. And very nearly groaned aloud when, seeing her, clearly having waited for her, Tony Johnstone stepped out of the shadows.

'You didn't phone!' he accused. 'Your father said you would, but you didn't.'

Her father had obviously told him where they would be that night too. 'Tony I...' was as far as she got before she realised that she had not left the restaurant on her own.

'Are you going to introduce your friend, Jazzlyn?' Holden asked coolly.

'I'm her boyfriend,' Tony stated aggressively, before she could get her head together.

'Not tonight, you're not,' Holden told him shortly. 'Tonight Miss Palmer is with me!'

'But I've waited here for...' Tony began to protest.

Only Holden, it seemed, had no intention of arguing, and before Tony could finish Holden had caught a hold of Jazzlyn by her arm and, giving her time only to see Tony's crestfallen expression, placed himself in between the two of them, marching her over to the car parking area.

That annoyed Jazzlyn. She was used to making her own decisions about what, why and wherefore, and whom she spoke to and where she wanted to go. 'That wasn't necessary! she snapped as they came to a halt beside his sleek car—Tony had obviously taken the hint that his presence was not required, because he was nowhere about.

'Did I not hear you myself, nine days ago, telling the ''boyfriend'' that he was now your *ex*-boyfriend?' Holden questioned curtly.

So he *had* remembered! 'That's got nothing to do with it—he looked hurt. I could have handled it better!'

'That's why he's still around, is it? Still teasing the poor sap?'

Poor sap! Because Tony thought he wanted to marry her! *'Teasing!'* she exploded. 'I was straight with him. I...'

'So was I!' Holden bit. Then added silkily, 'Forgive my over-protective mistake. I rather thought you...'

'Over-protective!' she exclaimed—and that was when suddenly everything fell into place. Jazzlyn wasn't thinking of herself then, because in a blinding kind of flash she all at once knew the answer to something that had been ferreting away in the back of her mind those past nine days. 'You're over-protective of your aunt too, aren't you?' she accused sharply.

'My aunt!' he echoed, as though not quite with her, or the unexpected change of direction the conversation had taken. But Jazzlyn didn't doubt for a moment that he was perfectly aware of what she was talking about.

'You didn't call the other Wednesday about Grace's birthday dinner at all, did you?' she accused, highly offended on her father's behalf, and deeply embarrassed on her own. 'You called to—to inspect my father! To check on him, to investigate, to give him the once-over!' She paused for breath, glaring at him.

In that well-lit car park Holden Hathaway stared back at her. He was in no way abashed and leaned back, refusing to look away. 'And if I did?' he questioned.

'You're despicable!' she exploded. 'How dare you invite my father to dine with you? How dare you invite *me* along as well?' she flew.

'I dare because my aunt's well being, especially after what she's previously endured, is important to me!' he rapped, and flicked his angry gaze from her only when they first heard and then saw Grace Craddock and Edwin Palmer coming across the car park towards them. 'And if you've half the regard you seem to have for my aunt, you'll keep your hot-headed temper to yourself and allow this birthday evening to end as pleasantly for her as it began,' he snarled in an aggressive undertone.

Jazzlyn threw him a withering look—which didn't so much as dent him, but more bounced off without the slightest effect—and turned from him. Arrogant toad! There was so much more she wanted to hurl at him, but he was right, dammit. This was his aunt's evening.

Jazzlyn moved from him, and as he opened the front passenger door for her she opened the rear one and got into the back seat. Bite her tongue she might, but there was no way she was going to drive home sitting next to the overbearing, over-protective swine!

CHAPTER TWO

HOT-HEADED—*her*? Only since she had known *him*, Jazzlyn fumed, more than once over the weekend that followed. Never, so far as she could remember, had she ever let fly at anybody the way she had gone for him.

And didn't she have cause! Arrogant devil! Him and his 'Tonight Miss Palmer is with me.' He'd said it every bit as if she should be grateful! Could he go and take a running jump. Who did he think he was, the lofty swine? Until she'd met him she hadn't had a hot-headed bone in her body!

Jazzlyn was feeling decidedly out of sorts, and her feeling of being just a tiny bit fed up with her lot was not helped when Tony Johnstone pestered her with phone calls both Saturday and Sunday.

'Look, Tony, you really must stop phoning—or writing to me,' she added hastily, wanting no communication from him whatsoever.

'You've got a new boyfriend now!' he accused. 'You don't care that I'm eating my heart out over you.'

'Tony, please!' This was dreadful. 'I don't want to hurt your feelings, honestly I don't, but there's no point at all in our talking.' Jazzlyn paused, took a deep breath and said very gently, 'I'm not going to go out with you again.'

Much good did it do her. He phoned again Monday, and she wasn't sure that she didn't spot him outside her place of work at lunchtime on Tuesday. He phoned that evening when she got in.

Her father, who was vague at the best of times and at others mostly in his own world, knew nothing of this. But Grace, who arrived on Wednesday to spend another few days with them, did. Grace was there when Jazzlyn arrived home on Wednesday, and she saw the hunted look on Jazzlyn's face when the phone rang.

'Is Tony still calling you' she asked sympathetically.

'Like—daily,' Jazzlyn answered worriedly. 'I shall have to answer it,' she sighed, 'or he'll disturb Dad.'

'Shall I take it?' Grace offered.

It was tempting, but Jazzlyn shook her head, wishing Grace's conviction that he would soon get tired of his unrequited pursuit would show some signs of being proved right—but there didn't seem to be much hope of that. In fact it seemed worse, not better. The call *was* from Tony, and again Jazzlyn came away from the phone feeling emotionally frazzled.

'What you need,' Grace opined as they talked it over, 'is to get away for a while.'

'Bliss!' Just the thought of being somewhere where Tony and his unwanted attentions couldn't reach her was starting to sound like pure and utter Shangri-La.

'Couldn't you take some time off from the office just now?' Grace pressed.

'I suppose I could. I do have plenty of my holiday entitlement unused.' She could, she mused, go and spend some time with her grandparents, but she'd stayed a weekend with them only recently. And anyhow, to disappear for a while suddenly seemed a cowardly thing to do. 'I'll stick it out,' she decided. 'I'm certain he's not truly in love with me. He's just let slip—in the context of it being the real thing this time—that he's already been engaged several times. I'm sure, as you suggested, it won't be long before he gets tired.' She wondered who she was trying to convince.

'You don't think you should perhaps tell your father…?'

Jazzlyn shook her head. 'No need for us all to be worried. I wouldn't have worried you with it, only…'

'Only I was here and saw for myself you were having an unpleasant time of it,' Grace ended for her.

Jazzlyn's affection for Grace, already warm, cemented from then on, but she was at her desk on Thursday morning when thoughts of Holden Hathaway interrupted her morning's work. She owned that it had happened before—thoughts of him intruding—but today, most likely because she was starting to feel protective of Grace too, Jazzlyn was able to think of him without getting all steamed up.

That had been some 'hot-headedness' she acknowledged, in that it had taken almost a

week for her to cool down and to start to see—
as in all fairness she had to—that perhaps
Holden had a point. Grace was sweet, and to
have been married to a womaniser for thirty
years before she had seen fit to divorce him
showed that she was either gullible or open to
being used as a doormat, possibly both. If
Grace was her aunt wouldn't she, given the
same circumstances, want to personally check
out any new, potentially long-term relationship
she embarked on too?

Jazzlyn knew that Grace came from monied
people. And, while Edwin Palmer wasn't poor,
he wasn't exactly rolling in it either. Also, although it was plain to anyone who saw them
together that Grace and her father were extremely comfortable and content with each
other, there was no getting away from the fact
that Edwin Palmer had, as well as having been
married three times, had many testy and un-
sustainable 'friendships'. Women liked him,
and Grace plainly trusted him. But only
Jazzlyn could have assured anyone interested
that, while obviously liking women, her father
was not a deceiver. He would never lie to or
cheat on anyone.

She went home from her office that night feeling more like her old self—though not relishing the early evening phone call which she was certain would come. It did. But when she took Rembrandt off for a walk strangely it was not Tony that she thought of but the man who last Friday had accused her of having a hot temper.

Grace went home on Friday morning and Jazzlyn returned from her office that evening a little later than usual, to hear the phone ring. She fed Rembrandt his usual biscuit treat, hoping the ringing would stop. But it didn't and, rather than have her father disturbed, she went to answer it.

'Yes!' she snapped. She didn't know how much more of this she could take. She was growing heartily weary of the whole Tony Johnstone business!

'Shall I ring back another time?' queried a pleasant voice that wasn't Tony's but was a voice she knew immediately.

'I'm sorry, I thought it was someone else,' she apologised straight away. 'I'm afraid your aunt isn't here; she went home this morning. Er—that is Holden, isn't it?'

'Have you forgiven me yet?' he asked, his charm quite flooring her.

Jazzlyn swallowed. Really, there was just something about this man which sometimes did devastating things to her equilibrium. 'It's I who should ask forgiveness,' she answered honestly. 'On thinking about it, I've realised that if Grace was my aunt, and stood the smallest chance of being duped, I'd want to find out a little more about the new man she appeared to be going steady with.'

There was a small silence at the other end, and then, almost involuntarily it seemed, Holden Hathaway murmured, 'What a lovely creature you are!'

Her heart fluttered crazily because it seemed, with her honesty, she had gained Holden's good opinion. 'Hey!' she exclaimed, well aware he could be a brute if the mood was on him. 'Don't get carried away!'

She heard him laugh. It was a pleasing sound, but not prolonged, and his tone was even when he corrected her assumption. 'I didn't ring to speak to Grace.'

'My father?' she questioned sharply.

'Put your hackles down,' he drawled. 'You,' he said.

'You rang to speak to me?' Her heart gave that crazy flutter again. Ridiculous. 'What about?' she demanded.

'I need a partner for a dinner-dance it seems I have to attend tomorrow evening,' he stated. He was asking her to go to a dinner-dance with him! Feeling momentarily stunned, while being aware he must be waiting for her to say something, Jazzlyn had no reply. She had thought of staying home, had already turned down a date with one of the newly qualified solicitors at her office. But—Holden Hathaway asking her out? Was that a surprise! 'I thought of you,' he went on, when nothing came from her but utter silence, 'because I know you're safe.'

Safe! What the heck did that mean? 'Safe?' she queried, nowhere near to working out what he meant by 'safe'. Though first, it seemed, he wanted confirmation that he had got the situation accurately assessed.

'I am right in thinking that you're not in the smallest way interested in any long-term relationship?' he checked.

Jazzlyn still had no clue to where this was leading, but saw no harm in giving him the confirmation he appeared to require. 'Most definitely,' she assured him.

'Good!' He sounded relieved! She was starting to feel a tiny bit miffed. What twenty-two-year-old wanted to be called 'safe'? 'The thing is,' he went on to explain, 'I'm obliged to attend this social function—and there's someone else attending whom I wouldn't mind knowing that my attentions are otherwise engaged.'

Safe? It clicked! 'A woman, obviously.' Why did she feel a shade peeved. 'You want to make her jealous!'

'The opposite, actually.' Plainly he was being pursued.

'I'd have thought you could handle a woman in hot pursuit,' Jazzlyn offered dryly.

'Correct me if I'm wrong, but that *was* Tony of ''Tony I've enjoyed your company but I won't be going out with you again'' who was skulking around hoping for a glimpse of you last Friday?'

He really was a swine! 'Touché!' she granted—and realised he must be having a problem similar to her own.

'So, to save me from feminine clutches—and to show you forgive me—will you partner me tomorrow night?' he asked handsomely.

Jazzlyn caved in. 'You've charm enough to sink a battleship!' she informed him. She was aware now that just by being there last Friday he had, so to speak, saved her from Tony's clutches, and she felt she would do as he asked. 'One thing, though—this lady, the one you're trying not to impress, her—um—heart isn't truly involved, is it?'

'You're a softie!' he murmured. But he gave her the assurance she wanted. 'I promise you her main interest is in my wallet.'

'You don't seem to care.'

'Like you, I'm seldom without my sprinting shoes.'

'Will you call for me, or shall I meet you somewhere?' Her acceptance of partnering him was implicit in her answer.

'I'll call for you at seven,' he replied, and she felt sure there was a smile in his voice at her agreement to go with him.

Idiotically, she found that she was smiling too. Though not for long. No sooner had she put the phone down than it rang again. It was

Tony. She dealt with him, and took Rembrandt for a walk, and wondered, feeling a touch despairing, if Holden was having the same sort of daily telephone hassle?

She was out with Rembrandt for some while, and was glad to be feeling a bit better on the way home. Her thoughts then were more centred on Holden than on Tony. She guessed, with Holden saying that he was obliged to attend the dinner-dance, that it must have something to do with business. Now what was she going to wear?

Jazzlyn could never remember having paid so much attention to her appearance before. But as she got ready the following evening she grew ever more certain the other females in the party would be very smartly turned out. She wanted to look her best. Her straight-skirted full-length black velvet gown was perfectly plain but showed off her slender waist and neat curves admirably. The neckline, while being decorous, was, she felt, a touch on the low side, and exposed the pale, almost translucent skin of her throat and chest with a delicate hint of cleavage. Jazzlyn relieved the bareness with the single strand of pearls her father had given her on her eighteenth birthday. Her white-blonde hair she pulled back from her face and piled on top of her head in a wavy kind of knot.

She had told her father of Holden's phone call, explaining that it wasn't a date as such and that Holden had thought of her when he'd needed a partner at short notice. She hadn't told her father of her own problems with an ex-date; it hardly seemed fair that she should tell him of Holden's.

'Will I do?' she asked her father when she went down to the sitting room, adding quickly, 'Stay, Remmy!' when the dog got up and looked as if he would come over—much as she loved him, she didn't fancy dog hair all over the black velvet of her dress.

Her father grabbed hold of the dog's collar just to be sure. 'You look a picture,' he smiled. 'I'm a very lucky man to have a daughter who has an inner beauty as well as beauty on the outside.'

'Oh, that's a lovely thing to say,' Jazzlyn said softly.

'It's true,' Edwin Palmer answered. It was very rarely that he spoke of her mother but he went on, 'Your mother had it.' He paused. 'Grace has it too,' he added. And Jazzlyn knew then that she, her mother and Grace were all very special to him.

'Be happy,' she said, and they both heard a car pull up.

'That's my wish for you,' he said. 'Tell Holden I won't come out; I'm busy holding on to the mutt.'

She laughed. 'See you when I see you,' she said, and felt suddenly in quite a flutter as she went out into the hall. So much so that, with no one there to see her, she had to pause to take several deep breaths.

The doorbell pealed. She steadied herself, then went to answer it. She had known a moment or two of anxiety, wondering if her dress was a little over the top, but, seeing Holden immaculate and a shade overwhelming in a crisp white shirt and dinner suit, she felt she had made the right choice.

As she stared at him, a man who seemed to her just then to most unfairly have it all, she suddenly realised that he was staring at her. 'Stunning!' he murmured softly. 'You look positively stunning.'

'I w-won't let you down?' she asked a touch nervously.

'Jazzlyn Palmer, you're a delight,' he smiled, and at such charm she was momentarily spellbound.

But she was made of sterner stuff, and quickly recovered. 'I'll take that as a no,' she laughed, adding, 'My father's holding the dog.'

'I'm pleased to hear it.'

They both laughed, and on the way to the car Jazzlyn explained about the adorable loose wiry-haired mongrel who had adopted them, and why she wasn't inviting him in to say hello to her father.

As Holden steered his car down the drive, however, it suddenly hit Jazzlyn that he might have thought his aunt was staying with them, and that he might have wanted to have a word of greeting with her.

'Grace isn't with us this weekend,' she said in a rush.

'Your father's calling for her later,' Holden replied, seeming straight away to tune on to her wavelength.

'Do you know everything?'

He gave her a sideways smile. 'Apparently sisters ferret everything out about each other.'

'You've been phoning your mother again.'

She thought she might have offended him with that remark, but that sideways smile suddenly became a most devastating grin, 'My mother phoned me,' he replied.

And doubtless she had wanted to know what he thought of her sister's artist friend. Jazzlyn felt she just had to assure him in some small way. 'Try not to worry about Grace too much.' His grin had disappeared—not a good sign. Feeling she was rushing in where angels might fear to tread, Jazzlyn just had to carry on, 'My father—your aunt—Grace is very special to him, you know,' she assured him.

'He told you this, did he?'

Was the edge going off his humour? Oh Lord, she wished she'd kept quiet; this was a fine way to start the evening. 'Not in so many words,' she replied stiffly.

'How, then, do you know?'

'I just do!' she flared—what was it about this man? She even felt compelled to continue—and that too annoyed her. 'If you must know, my father was talking about inner beauty. He said that my mother had inner beauty, and then, unprompted, he said Grace had inner beauty too.'

'He's the artist—he'd see beneath the surface more than most, I'd imagine.'

'My father doesn't lie—he's very sincere!' she stated categorically.

And had her breath taken away when he dared to remind her. 'And has three marriages behind him to prove it.'

'You *rat*!' she exploded, and was in two minds whether to tell him to turn the car around immediately.

'Did I say "hot-headed"?' Holden muttered—and, not knowing what it was about this man, Jazzlyn just had to laugh. 'So you're not going to forsake me?' he questioned, clearly having realised she'd been on the point of telling him he could go to his wretched dinner-dance on his own.

'Mind-reader!' she muttered—and *he* laughed.

By unspoken mutual consent, neither her father nor his aunt were referred to again on that journey, and good humour was totally restored by the time Holden was escorting her through the smart portals of a most salubrious hotel.

Prior to arriving at the hotel, Jazzlyn had admitted to herself that she was feeling a little nervous about the evening. But now, unsure if it was just being with him—or what it was— she discovered from almost the first moment that she began to feel completely at ease.

That Holden was popular was obvious because many people came up to greet him and to be introduced to his companion. He was attentive to her, and Jazzlyn realised that he was letting it be known that she was his date. She guessed that the female whose clutches he wanted to avoid without causing offence— probably some business associate—would know it too.

But, though he made it known that she was with him, that did not prevent several other men in the party from staying over-long in her vicinity. Nor, when they were seated at dinner, did Holden's presence on one side of her prevent the man on the other side from engaging her in frequent conversation.

'Is Brian Fox bothering you?' Holden bent to ask considerately in her ear at one stage.

She smiled at Holden for his concern—when he took a girl out, he took a girl out! No leaving her to struggle on. Though how he could do anything about it, seated as they all were, she didn't know. She just knew that do something he would. But his concern was unnecessary.

'He's most interesting to talk with,' she replied honestly. And then, with her usual honesty, as laughter bubbled up inside her, 'You're not feeling neglected, are you?'

He laughed at her for her sauce—and turned his attention to the elegant woman sitting on the other side of him. So there! But Jazzlyn wasn't offended; she reckoned she'd asked for that and she gave Holden the benefit of her shoulder as she turned away and leaned forward too as the man opposite engaged her in conversation.

The meal was very enjoyable, but by the time the coffee was served Jazzlyn was still no nearer to discerning whom Holden's wallet-attracted female was. She had observed many women in the party giving him a second and a third look—but while several of the women seemed to hang on his every word no female was actually drooling. But these were sophisticated people. Perhaps sophisticated people didn't drool!

Music was being played, and she saw one of the younger men in the group leave his seat. Her attention was distracted by Holden, who had seen the man making his way over too. 'I think, for the look of the thing, you'd better have the first dance with me,' he decreed, getting to his feet.

Jazzlyn supposed, without being sure of the whys and wherefores of such matters, that he was right. She made to move and Holden pulled her chair back—and just then the other man reached them. 'I was just about to ask you for a dance!' the man complained, fixing his eyes on Jazzlyn.

'Sorry, Lewin, your timing's out,' Holden addressed him before she could find her tongue.

'I shall return,' he promised.

'I'd love to dance with you later.' Jazzlyn felt sorry for Mr Lewin, having circumnavigated the table only to receive this sort of reception, and thought it just too rude to walk by him without so much as a word.

She and Holden were on the dance floor and he had placed an arm around her when he commented, 'No wonder you have trouble dumping your men!'

Jazzlyn looked up in surprise, meeting his steady grey eyes full on. 'Was I too encouraging?' she asked, her lovely violet eyes wide and worried.

He stared down at her. 'Oh, Jazzlyn, Jazzlyn,' he said softly, and pulled her close, out of a nearby dancing couple's way, his gaze holding hers.

Her heart suddenly started to hammer, and her lips parted as a warm light came into his eyes—eyes that searched her face, flicked down to her throat and the pale expanse of her chest and on to the shadowed parting of her breasts. Swiftly then he looked back to her parted lips and up into her violet eyes.

He looked away—and when, having danced her into a less congested area, he looked down at her again, it was with that same steady look, and Jazzlyn knew that she had imagined that warm light in his eyes. 'You don't have to do anything to encourage a man,' he teased in a light, matter-of-fact kind of way. 'Most men would fall over themselves to get near to you just for your looks alone.'

Most men, but not you, she found herself thinking, deciding there and then that she was never going to go out with him again. Then, as she all at once realised the direction in which her thinking was going, she pulled herself up short. Good grief, this wasn't a proper date! Nor did she want it to be! And, for goodness' sake, she didn't want Holden falling over himself to get near her. But no, she would not go out with him again—even if he did ask her—which he wouldn't. She had enough problems dealing with the likes of Tony Johnstone in her life without dating again a tall, dark-haired sophisticated man of the world like Holden Hathaway!

'Thank you,' he said. She glanced up at him—the music had stopped.

'Duty done,' she said of the dance, but as they went back to their table his arm was no longer around her and his left hand no longer held hers. It was only then that she was able to deny that her heart had beat in any way other than its natural rhythm when she had been held by him.

The man Holden had addressed as Lewin did get to dance with her, as did several other males of the party. But, although Jazzlyn saw Holden dancing with one or two of the other women, he did not ask her to dance again. And that, she told herself, she was glad about.

'Unless you particularly want to stay, I think we can go now,' Holden commented as she came off the floor after a third dance with Paul Lewin.

'Anything you say,' she answered agreeably.

'I've enjoyed your company,' he offered as, having said their goodbyes, they went out to his car.

'I've enjoyed yours,' she replied easily. 'That meal was a bit special, wasn't it?'

'Lewin asked for your phone number, of course?'

'Of course.'

They were in Holden's car, the hotel five minutes away behind them, when Holden asked casually, 'Did you give it to him?'

She could have asked him what in creation he was talking about, but uncannily she felt right on Holden's wavelength. 'I wasn't sure how seriously you and I were supposed to be attached,' she answered, knowing that Holden would know from that that she *hadn't* parted with her phone number.

'Did you want him to have it?' he questioned easily.

She shook her head, then realised Holden was concentrating on the road up ahead and hadn't seen her negative action. 'No,' she said, adding with a light laugh, 'I'd like to clear up present problems before I date anybody again.'

'Rex?'

'Rex Alford isn't a problem. He's no more serious than I am. I've been out with him a couple of times, and he's good fun. But... Which lady was it—tonight? The one you were trying to...?'

'I know I'm being unfair, but to tell you isn't in the ethical code of gentlemanly behavior.'

'That *is* unfair! You know all about my love-life!'

'I doubt that I do,' he answered smoothly. 'Was it Tony you were expecting to call when I rang last night?' he questioned before she could blink.

'Despite my telling him—repeatedly—that I'm not interested, he rings every night.'

'He hasn't got the message yet?'

'Apparently not.'

'What does your father say—about you being pestered with these unwanted phone calls every night?' Holden asked.

'I haven't told him!'

'You don't think you should?'

'I don't think it will go on for much longer. Tony Johnstone's been engaged several times, which makes me fairly sure he's a bit fickle in the heart department. I'm sure he'll soon get tired—it's just wearing while it's going on, that's all. Grace knows, and...'

'You've told her?'

'Oh, not to worry her,' Jazzlyn assured him. 'Grace has just happened to be around a few times when Tony's phoned.' Jazzlyn paused, then added quietly, 'I'm—grateful to be able to talk things over with her.'

'I'm glad,' Holden offered kindly, and Jazzlyn knew he wasn't upset on his aunt's behalf. 'Your mother died when you were small, I believe?' he followed up.

'I was five and staying overnight with my grandparents when my parents were in a traffic accident that should never have happened.' Bearing in mind that she had been ready to end the evening before it had begun when she'd felt Holden had been particularly acid about her father, Jazzlyn hesitated to tell him of her grandparents' view that Katherine Palmer's death had left her father in a stunned state of shock for months, and that when he had eventually come out of it his whole personality seemed to have changed. Live now, pay later, had seemed to be his motto then. 'My father was—different after that,' Jazzlyn began, not seeing why, when she had been open and honest all her life, she should start minding her words now. 'According to my grandparents, while the shock of losing his beloved Katherine sent him into a no man's land where nobody could reach him, that same shock changed him from a home-loving dreamer into some kind of live-for-the-moment man. Why am I telling you all this?' she asked abruptly.

'Defiance, I shouldn't wonder,' Holden drawled, and Jazzlyn just had to be amused. For some unknown reason she felt just then that she could make a friend of this straight-forward man.

'So I'll shut up. Only—only...' Again she hesitated.

'You're not going coy on me now, are you?' Holden prompted.

'Wouldn't dream of it. I just thought, bearing in mind how protective you are of your aunt, that you might like to know that my father hates portrait work.'

'I'll bear it in mind,' Holden replied solemnly.

Jazzlyn gave him an exasperated look, but after a moment ploughed on anyway. 'So, draw from it what you will, but, while my father has done several portraits of me over the years, the only other non-commissioned portraits he has painted are those of my mother and your aunt.

'You're reiterating that my aunt is very special to him?' Holden questioned evenly.

Jazzlyn felt a degree or two of frost in the air. 'Would I dare?' she offered sniffily. And, suddenly feeling a need to give him a verbal battering, she continued, 'You didn't hurt her feelings, I trust?'

'My aunt's?'

'The female I was protecting you from to-night,' Jazzlyn supplied sweetly—and wanted to thump him when his mood went in an instant from chilly to good-humoured.

'Did I mention—you're a delight?' he asked.

She didn't want to be flattered, knew that it was only his charm and he meant nothing truly personal by it, but she could do nothing at all, however, about the inner bubble of laughter she felt inside, or the fact that her laughter should manifest itself in the upward curve of her lips. She stared away from him at the grass verge illuminated in the car's headlights.

It seemed that any animosity between them had totally evaporated by the time Holden was turning into the driveway of her home. He drew the car to a halt and walked to the door with her, taking the key from her hand and inserting it in the lock.

'Thank you for being such a good companion,' he acknowledged appreciatively.

'I enjoyed myself,' she answered sunnily—and then suddenly, as Holden's head started to come nearer and her heart began to race erratically, she knew he was going to kiss her! He did kiss her—on her cheek. A warm sensitive, brief, *chaste* kiss—she might have been his maiden aunt!

'Goodnight, Jazzlyn,' he bade her matter-of-factly, and pushed the door inwards.

'Goodnight,' she answered lightly, and went in and closed the door. She was never, ever going to go out with him again! Her heart was still pounding. Oh, very definitely she wasn't going to go out with him again. Maiden aunt! Huh! Rembrandt came and thumped his tail against her legs—he cared not about black velvet. 'You're supposed to bark!' she told the bark-less hound, and, uncaring then of black velvet herself, she bent and gave him a hug, then went to bed.

By morning Jazzlyn was amazed by what had got into her last night. What on earth had come over her that she should be inwardly miffed that Holden should salute her cheek as if she were some maiden aunt? Grief, she'd have taken great exception had he saluted her in any other fashion. And as for her imagining that her heart had raced a little when she'd thought Holden about to kiss her on the lips—

pfff! As for going out with him again—he was unlikely to ask. Well, not unless he wanted protecting again! She grinned, her good humour restored. She spent a good deal of Sunday morning picking dog hair out of her dress.

Her good humour was dampened a little when Tony Johnstone phoned that evening. It was wearing, as she'd told Holden, tedious and upsetting, and she wished with all her heart that she had never gone out with Tony to start with.

By Tuesday—he had phoned again last night—Jazzlyn had run out of things to say to him. He rang as usual that night. She neither wanted to hurt his feelings nor tell her father and ask him to speak to him, but, she owned, she was really feeling the strain.

Tony rang again on Wednesday, refusing to listen to her entreaties to stop ringing her. But it was later, when she and her father were having a meal, that she realised she couldn't go on like this. She was starting to jump each time the telephone rang. Loath though she was to do it, she would have to enlist her father's help.

'Dad—' she began slowly—only he began at the same time.

'Grace rang today—' He broke off.

'You first,' she offered.

He accepted. 'I was speaking to Grace on the phone today.' Jazzlyn suspected that when Grace wasn't staying with them they spoke daily on the phone with each other. 'Grace was saying that, in view of the splendid long-range weather forecast, she was thinking of taking a fortnight's holiday in Hampshire.'

What Jazzlyn had been going to say went right out of her mind in her surprise. 'Without you?' she exclaimed.

'You're getting smart in your old age,' her father teased with a chuckle. 'We're going on Saturday.'

Her mouth fell open in surprise—her father seldom went on holiday! 'You'll have a lovely time,' she said, and felt sure they would. 'Have you booked your hotel yet?'

'We're not going to a hotel. Grace has been offered the loan of a very nice house. She's been there before, and apparently there's room enough for another little one.'

Jazzlyn stared at him. 'You want me to come with you?'

'I told Grace I'd teach her to sketch. I—er—thought you might like to look after Remmy while Grace and I go and draw some seascapes for a few hours.' A few hours! Her father lost all sense of time when he was out sketching! 'With you there I wouldn't have to worry about the dog running off into the sea when I'm not looking. Although I'd like you to come for your own sake, of course—if you can get the time off work. Grace would love you to come too.'

Jazzlyn hesitated. 'You're sure?'

'Of course I'm sure!'

'Two weeks, you said?'

'Pointless going for less,' Edwin Palmer opined.

Jazzlyn suddenly had horrific visions of Tony Johnstone ringing every night during the two weeks her father would be away. She could just about cope while she had the security of knowing that her father was in the house—but without him there? Jazzlyn knew she couldn't confide in him; not now he was going away. It wouldn't be fair. Would it be so cowardly of her to go away too? Surely if there was no one there to answer the phone Tony Johnstone would get fed up with calling before that two weeks was up? Two whole glorious phone-free weeks!

'It takes so much thinking about?' Edwin Palmer teased.

'Are you certain you and Grace want me with you?' Jazzlyn double-checked, suddenly seeing Grace and her father's generous offer as something of a lifeline.

'Don't be daft! Besides, I can't leave Rembrandt here by himself all day while you're at work—and he wouldn't be happy in kennels.'

He knew how to metaphorically twist her arm, did her father—though in truth she did not need the threat of their beloved hound being placed in kennels to make her accept. 'Oh, all right,' she agreed—and they both knew she was less reluctant than she appeared. 'For Remmy's sake I'll see if I can get some time off.'

Her immediate boss, Maurice Kyte, was a little put out that Jazzlyn wanted to take two weeks off at such short notice. But when she said that she appreciated two days' notice wasn't very much, and that she wouldn't go if he'd rather she didn't, he folded completely.

'You go,' he said. And, putting a good face on it, added, 'I'm going to have to put up with a temp whenever you go—perhaps it will be better to get your holiday arrangements over with now rather than later. Though I don't know how I'm going to manage without you,' he muttered, which was flattering.

'I'm sure you'll survive,' she smiled, but was already on to thinking that all *she* had to do was to survive another two phone calls from Tony—then she would be away.

Saturday dawned as bright and as sunny as the weathermen had forecast. Jazzlyn and her father had already debated whether to take one or two cars. It was his view that with his Range Rover being large enough for three of them and luggage, plus dog and dog basket, they should all go together in the one vehicle.

Grace had driven herself to the Palmer house the previous evening, so they set off early—Grace and Edwin Palmer at the front, Jazzlyn and Rembrandt in the rear. The further away they got from her Buckinghamshire home, the more relaxed Jazzlyn began to feel. But it was only as they neared the Hampshire village of Havorton that a feeling of well-being came to her, and only then did she fully appreciate how truly overstretched her nerves had been.

She had imagined Sandbanks to be a small holiday cottage. But as they turned up the driveway and she saw the large impressive three-storeyed house, she had to do a rapid re-think. Her father, when he'd told her that there was room for another little one, she realised, had put the notion into her head that the property Grace's friend had offered her the use of was tiny and seldom used. But in reality it was large enough to accommodate many more than the three of them and the dog. Proof that it was used more than just at holiday time was there in the fact that there was a resident housekeeper. Quite obviously Grace's well-to-do friends came from the same affluent background as Grace herself.

The housekeeper came out as they were unloading, and Jazzlyn saw when the housekeeper went straight to Grace that Grace was no stranger to Sandbanks. That was borne out when Grace introduced Mrs Williams to them.

The four of them and Rembrandt went indoors, and Grace, being familiar with the layout of the house, waited only for Mrs Williams to say that their rooms were ready before showing them upstairs to their sleeping quarters.

'This is your room, Jazzlyn' she smiled, opening a door along a wide and long landing to reveal a most beautifully appointed room.

'It's lovely!' Jazzlyn exclaimed sincerely. Going over to the window, she saw that from this part of the house there was a footpath which led straight down to the beach. 'I've a view of the sea!' she exclaimed in delight.

'I thought you might like it,' Grace answered, and Jazzlyn just had to go and give her a hug. She had an idea that Grace had phoned Mrs Williams and asked her to prepare this room especially for her.

After Grace had gone, Jazzlyn made short work of unpacking her case. Then, taking Rembrandt with her, she went to explore the beach and surrounds. Part of the beach was private to Sandbanks itself, she discovered, and quite close to the house lay a hilly clutch of sand dunes—a wonderful spot if ever one wanted a spot of splendid isolation, she felt. And rather wonderful even if one didn't.

Mrs Williams had said something about having a meal ready for them, so after a very short while, but promising herself she would explore further the next day, Jazzlyn called to Rembrandt and they returned to the house.

She slept better that night than she had in a long while, and woke up clear-headed and not oppressed by thoughts of Tony Johnstone. Though why the first person to pop into her thoughts was Holden Hathaway she had no clue—but she had to admit that it wasn't the first time he had entered her head unannounced.

Strangely enough, Holden Hathaway was there in her mind again when—her father and Grace having gone sketching—she and Rembrandt went off exploring. She supposed the reason for that was his uncanny ability to make her laugh inside, to make her smile and laugh at the most unexpected moment. She liked him, she had to admit—even if he did have a power like no other to make her cross.

'You're back!' she exclaimed to her father and Grace when much later she returned to the house to find them there.

'It was hot, and Grace forgot to take a sun hat,' Edwin Palmer answered, not a bit put out to have his morning's sketching abandoned, but more affectionately indulgent than anything.

Grace had already instructed Mrs Williams that since she was preparing a roast for the evening meal a few sandwiches would suffice for lunch. After the snack meal, Edwin Palmer murmured something about taking forty winks, and was teased, 'Shame on you!' by Grace. Then Grace said she thought she'd go for a walk.

'Would you like some company?' Jazzlyn asked.

'Love some!' Grace beamed.

Not many minutes later, and with Rembrandt now on a leash, they opted to take a walk around the pretty village of Havorton. 'This is a super spot,' Jazzlyn remarked as they strolled under the shade of overhanging trees.

'Feeling less uptight than you were?' Grace asked.

'Did it show?'

'A little,' Grace admitted.

'But not now—it sounds a bit dramatic, but I feel as though a great weight has been taken from me.'

'Good!' Grace responded, but added, 'Promise me that if the phone calls start up again when we get back, you'll allow your father to deal with it. He's stronger than you think, you know.'

'I—promise,' Jazzlyn agreed, and realised only then that her father *was* now strong, and that, amazingly, that strength, that look of having more of a purpose in life these days, had only come about since Grace had arrived in his life. Jazzlyn knew then that her father and Grace were good for each other.

They did a circuit of the village, and were just passing a close of houses prior to taking the lane that would lead them back to Sandbanks when the front door of one of the houses opened and a man of about thirty, carrying what looked like a doctor's bag, came walking down the garden path.

'Mrs Craddock!' he greeted Grace with obvious pleasure, though it was on Jazzlyn that his gaze rested.

'David, how nice to see you!' Grace smiled.

'How's the ankle?' He seemed in no hurry to rush off.

'As good as new,' Grace told him, and, turning to Jazzlyn, explained, 'David came to Sandbanks and strapped me up when I went over on my ankle about a year ago.' When the man showed a definite disinclination to move on, she introduced him, 'This is Dr Musgrove.'

'David, please.' He smiled at Jazzlyn.

'And this,' Grace continued as David Musgrove put out his right hand to shake Jazzlyn's, 'is Jazzlyn Palmer.'

'You're staying at Sandbanks too?' David asked Jazzlyn.

'We arrived yesterday,' Grace answered for her in friendly fashion.

'Not just for the weekend, I hope?'

'We've the prospect of two wonderful sun-drenched weeks,' Grace responded.

'Then I'll see you again,' he promised.

Rembrandt grew impatient and started pulling on his leash, and Jazzlyn, guessing that

Grace was ready to be on her way, smiled at the doctor. 'Bye,' she said, and she and Grace went on.

They were in the lane when Grace said, out of the blue, 'You know, of course, that David Musgrove is going to ask you for a date?'

Jazzlyn looked at her, startled. 'I didn't, actually,' she said, unsure if she wanted to go out with anybody again just yet—and why in creation should she also think of Holden? She banished him. 'But if he does...?'

'You'll be all right with him, Jazzlyn,' Grace assured her quietly.

Whether or not Grace was right that David Musgrove was going to ask her for a date, Jazzlyn had no idea. Though, while she was drying her newly washed hair at the fitted dryer in her adjoining bathroom the next morning, she gave the matter a little serious thought.

This was Grace's and her father's holiday too, and, while not truly believing that she had been roped in merely to play nursemaid to Rembrandt, Jazzlyn had no wish to play gooseberry either. She was sensitive to the fact that Grace and her father might want to relax in the evenings on their own. And, since they both might have something to say if she spent every evening watching television on the set in her bedroom, it might be an idea to accept an invitation to an evening out.

Grace seemed to be confident that she'd be all right with David Musgrove—and might it not do her good to go out with some new man? It might make Tony Johnstone more of a distant memory than he had already started to become, while at the same time—Jazzlyn faced it squarely—it would give her something else to think about other than the man who was much too frequently in her thoughts: Holden Hathaway.

Jazzlyn pushed Holden Hathaway out of her head and went down the stairs, silently amused. She was making all these plans as to whether or not to go on a date with David Musgrove—and he hadn't even been in touch yet!

He did get in touch. Just after breakfast. The phone rang and Grace went to answer it. 'For you,' she said, and, with an 'I told you so' grin, held the phone out to Jazzlyn.

Maurice Kyte, her employer, had her holiday phone number, but it would have to be some dire emergency before he used it. So, since David Musgrove was about the only other person who could know where to contact her, Jazzlyn guessed that of the two it would be him.

'Hello?' she queried.

'Hello, Jazzlyn. David Musgrove,' her caller announced himself.

'Oh, hello, David,' she answered, and saw Grace wait no longer than to be proved right before taking herself and Edwin Palmer out of earshot.

'I didn't think to ask yesterday if it was just you and Mrs Craddock taking a two-week break at Sandbanks?'

'We're here with my father, actually,' she answered openly.

'Just the three of you?'

She supposed that in his profession he liked to have everything double-checked. 'That's right,' she confirmed. 'It's a lovely spot, isn't it?'

'If you'd like to see more of it, I'd love to show you around.' He was in there as quick as a flash.

'I—er…' Why was she hesitating? Why did visions of a tall, dark-haired man with grey eyes come to her? Impatiently, she ousted Holden Hathaway from her head. 'Actually, I'm here as a dog-sitter-in-chief,' she prevaricated. 'I'm not sure you'd enjoy having our large, shaggy-haired hound in your car.'

'Are you dog-sitter-in-chief day *and* night?' Clearly he was not enamoured of the thought of having dog hair coating his upholstery, but was nevertheless not prepared to give up.

'No,' she owned.

'Then—would you come out to dinner with me one evening?' he asked.

She took a deep breath, thought of Holden and, annoyed that it should be so, said 'Yes.' She came away from the phone having agreed to go out with David Musgrove tomorrow evening, and feeling thoroughly mixed up. She supposed, in all honesty, that she had been going to accept a date with David anyway if he had indeed made contact, but she somehow felt she had been pushed into it by the lurking presence of Holden Hathaway.

Jazzlyn acquainted a waiting Grace with the details of her phone call, and waved her and her father off as they drove away to find a suitable sketching site. Then she took Rembrandt for a walk before it got too hot. When he started panting she took him back to Sandbanks, and Mrs Williams found him a cold tiled area near the kitchen, where he could flop, and turned a fan on him. He was in seventh heaven, but Jazzlyn realised she'd probably be walking without him while the beautiful weather held.

She went into the house to offer Mrs Williams any assistance she might need, but discovered that a young mother, Nancy, from the village, came to Sandbanks to help out on Mondays, Wednesdays and Fridays. Though her offer was appreciated, her help was not needed, so Jazzlyn collected a sketchpad of her own, and went to explore the sand dunes.

Edwin Palmer and Grace did not return at lunchtime, but Jazzlyn went back to the house to see that Rembrandt was not being a nuisance. Only to discover that he and Mrs Williams had become great friends—he was, it seemed, extremely partial to marzipan cake.

It seemed a shame to break up their mutual admiration society, so after a sandwich Jazzlyn took herself off again. She found some shade in the sand dunes—and let her thoughts drift.

'Did I mention,' he'd said, 'you're a delight?' So why didn't *he* ring and ask for a date? Other men did—not that she'd go out with him again! But she'd know she would be safe with him. Holden, like her, wasn't interested in being married, so... Oh, for goodness' sake get out of my head!

Realising that Holden was monopolising her thoughts again, and impatient with herself that it should be so, Jazzlyn left the sand dunes and headed for home. Right or left? She opted for left, towards the rear of the house, where the garages were, and had just strolled by the side of the house when, turning the corner, she stopped dead.

Was she seeing things? Was Holden Hathaway so dominating her thoughts that not only was he constantly in her head but she had taken to actually seeing him when he wasn't there? For she would swear that the long, sleek expensive car which had just pulled up at the rear of the house was his. And, astonishingly, that the man getting out of it was none other than—Holden Hathaway!

CHAPTER THREE

JAZZLYN, standing rooted in her tracks, realised that Holden was no apparition when just
then the housekeeper came out on some chore
and, seeing him, greeted him, her face full of
smiles.

With her heart beating a little faster, Jazzlyn
wondered what Holden was doing there. She
supposed it went without saying that he and
his aunt would know some of the same people.
And, since it was plain that he and the housekeeper were acquainted, perhaps he had stayed
at Sandbanks himself at some time or other.
Maybe his mother had mentioned in conversation where his aunt was, and maybe, finding
himself in the area, he had thought to stop by
for a cup of tea or something.

As the housekeeper moved to go back indoors Holden turned and spotted Jazzlyn. She
moved forward, realising that in his aunt's ab-
sence she would have to take on the role of
hostess.

Words sprang to her lips. 'Hello', 'Fancy seeing you here', 'Well, look who the wind blew in', but, as Holden stood there watching her draw closer, none of it got said. Just then they both heard the sound of the Range Rover—and Jazzlyn was never more pleased. Holden, plainly having business in this area, was immaculately suited, while she, dressed in shorts and a baggy shirt, had been grubbing around in the sand dunes—and couldn't remember when last she'd pulled a comb through her hair.

Feeling certain she looked a mess, she smiled at Holden. 'How's it going?' she greeted him as the Range Rover turned the corner into view.

'No complaints,' he answered, his sophisticated glance travelling over her urchin-like appearance. 'Yourself?'

'Having a wonderful time!' she bounced back, the words 'glad that you're here' coming unbidden to mind. 'Er—here's your aunt and my father,' she added unnecessarily. She felt a mass of confusion suddenly, as Holden took his eyes away from her and turned to watch his delighted aunt, 'Excuse me,' Jazzlyn added—and bolted.

She was upstairs in her room before she had space enough to wonder what was going on. What the dickens was the matter with her? Grief, Holden wasn't the only sophisticated man she was acquainted with!

Oh, heck, why had she bolted like that? All she'd done now was give herself a problem. Because, lack of courtesy aside—even if Holden had come to see his aunt and not her— she couldn't stay up here in her room for the duration of his visit. She would have to go down and pass a few words with the company in general while they drank tea, prior to making a graceful and tactful exit so that, should Holden wish to discuss family matters, he could have some private conversation with his aunt.

Grabbing up her brush, she went to work on her hair—oh, help, she hadn't a scrap of make-up on! She dashed to the bathroom and washed her face—and then realised that Holden might be forgiven for thinking he had some effect on her if the next time he saw her she was wearing a full 'paint-job'—not that she normally wore much make-up anyway.

It was at that point that Jazzlyn stood stock still and got herself together. Never, she realised, had she ever got herself into such a state over a man before. But that was all he was—a man. A nephew. A nephew who had dropped by to see his aunt. Out of politeness, she would go down and see him—shame it was so hot. To take Rembrandt for a walk would have been a splendid excuse to get out of there.

Five minutes later, having wondered what in creation she needed an excuse for, Jazzlyn, having resorted to the merest trace of lipstick and changed into a pair of white trousers and a sleeveless top, left her room.

As she had anticipated, all three were in the drawing room, with Holden's aunt presiding over the teacups. Holden rose to his feet and Jazzlyn, hoping he had no recollection of what she had been wearing, quickly subsided into the nearest chair.

'Tea?' Grace enquired with a smile.

'No thanks.' Jazzlyn smiled back. If a convenient moment occurred, she wanted to be able to get up and leave without being hindered by a half-drunk cup of tea. 'How did the sketching go?' she asked.

'Could do better!' Grace laughed, and added, 'Help me persuade my nephew to take a few days off. He's just admitted he has no reason to return to London and could take a break.' And while Jazzlyn, inwardly startled, realised that Grace must mean for Holden to stay there—with them—his aunt was turning to him and, in loving-aunt fashion, continuing, 'You work so hard, Holden. A short rest from it will do you no harm whatsoever.'

'And you'd be excellent company for Jazzlyn.' Edwin Palmer put his size thirteens in it, and Jazzlyn, who seldom had a cross word with her parent, was exceedingly annoyed. For crying out loud—she didn't need him or anyone else drumming up boyfriends for her! How *could* he?

Annoyance fused with embarrassment, and, as she felt three pairs of eyes zero in on her, Jazzlyn just couldn't stay seated. 'I'd better take a look at Rembrandt,' she remarked generally, not having anticipated leaving the room so soon—but really, there *were* limits. 'He's been with Mrs Williams most of the day; I don't want him to be a nuisance,' she added, making for the door.

Rembrandt had moved slightly since last she'd seen him, but he was still in the cold tiled area and Mrs Williams, far from seeming as if she was fed up with the hound, seemed more smitten than ever.

'Not a bit of trouble. He's as good as gold,' she answered when Jazzlyn asked if he'd been any trouble. 'He likes that little spot,' she suggested.

Jazzlyn took the hint and left him where he was, but she could no more return to the drawing room than fly. She went out by a rear door and was still feeling upset ten minutes later when, with her hands dug in her trouser pockets, she wandered along the beach. Honestly! She was her father's greatest fan. But *really*!

Impatiently, peeved and embarrassed, she half turned—and nearly died! Holden, having shed the jacket of his suit and his tie, was walking towards her.

She had two choices—run, or wait. Dignity settled the issue. She waited. 'Still upset?' he enquired easily, as he drew close.

He saw too much! She had thought she'd hidden her embarrassment, her discomfiture, but apparently this man missed nothing. Holden stopped about a yard away from her and she eyed him solemnly, too honest to pretend she didn't know what he meant.

'I've enough problems getting rid of present men-friends without my father soliciting new ones for me!' she answered shortly.

'What did I do?' he asked at her tone, as well he might, for he had done nothing. But she was not to be teased out of her discomfiture and so, having not taken the smallest offence at her tone, Holden reasoned quietly, 'I don't think your father truly meant it that way.' He added, 'But, either way, he doesn't know about our special relationship.'

Jazzlyn shot a glance up at him, her violet eyes staring. It actually felt as if her heart had missed a beat at those words 'our special relationship'. 'Of course,' she mumbled, as his meaning penetrated, and suddenly she started to feel a whole lot better. She had gone out with Holden on the understanding that it was so he could keep some wallet-inclined female at arm's length. But, as Holden had assumed, her father hadn't known that. And so, with Holden turning up today, her father—never the best mathematician—had probably put two and two together and made five.

'You're much too sensitive,' Holden commented, and her heart raced again.

She looked away from him and found she was having to search quite desperately for something sensible to say. 'It's too hot for Remmy.' She shared that semi-sensible snippet with him.

'In that case we won't play it,' Holden answered—and she burst out laughing. She just had to.

'Remmy is Rembrandt—the dog!' she informed him, her sweet mouth curving upwards as she looked up at Holden again.

He stared down at her, his eyes on her mouth—before he transferred his gaze to her eyes. 'Pals?' he asked. 'Are we friends, Jazzlyn?'

She wanted to be friends with him. Somehow she had a feeling that she never wanted to have a cross word with him. 'Friends,' she agreed, and held out her hand.

He took it, his right hand covering her dainty right hand. 'How do you feel about your friend staying on at Sandbanks for a few days?' he asked.

She looked at him, her expression at once serious. 'You're welcome to stay with us,' she replied.

'That wasn't what I asked,' he reproved.

Staring up at him, she knew truthfulness was the only way. 'I'd love my pal to stay,' she told him honestly.

Holden looked down at her, and—as a friend—gently touched her lips with his. Her heart thumped crazily, but even as he took a step away and let go her hand, that whisper of a kiss plainly affecting him not the slightest, Holden was asking casually, 'Still being badgered by the limpet Tony?'

By mutual consent they began to stroll back to the house, and Jazzlyn sought and found the light sort of note she wanted as she answered, 'I don't seem to be getting through to him.'

'Want me to go and beat him up?' Holden offered lightly.

Laughter bubbled up inside her. 'You don't think that would be just a mite *too* subtle?' she enquired, laughter in her eyes. She glanced at him and saw that his eyes were alight with laughter too.

Holden was buttonholed by his aunt when they reached the house, so Jazzlyn parted from him and went up to her room. She was happy, she realised. Happy that Holden was there.

Because Holden was there? That notion worried her for a short while, until she was able to satisfactorily conclude why wouldn't she be happy he was there—in a manner of speaking, he was family! Not only was he her friend, but he was Grace's nephew.

Jazzlyn wasn't at all sure how she felt when she found she was going on to contemplate Holden's relationship to her in the context of—what if Grace and her father were to marry?

It was a sobering thought—and one which she didn't want to face. Grace was totally different from her father's previous two wives, of course, but... No, she didn't want to think about it.

Though if—and a very big 'if' it was too—her father married Holden's aunt, that would make her and Holden almost related, wouldn't it? Jazzlyn found she was happier puzzling over what her official relationship to Holden would be than in thinking on the subject of marriage.

Wouldn't that, though, in the event of her father trying for happiness for a fourth time, make Grace her stepmother and Holden a kind of step-cousin? Jazzlyn found she quite liked the idea of having a step-cousin.

But, having no experience of such matters, having no cousins—step or otherwise—she couldn't help but wonder as she looked for something to wear if it was usual for a female maybe step-cousin to be so bothered about what to put on to share dinner with her newly arrived male maybe step-cousin? She didn't remember being so bothered about what to wear last night.

She decided that, since probably all Holden had with him were the business clothes he stood up in, for all she was on holiday she would wear a pair of smart black trousers and a white silk shirt. Why she should match her wardrobe to suit his she had no idea—perhaps, as he'd said, she was a touch sensitive.

Jazzlyn later went down the stairs, musing that possibly Holden intended to go into town tomorrow and purchase some casual clothes. But when she went into the drawing room she saw with surprise that he had no need to. For, broad-shouldered and manly, Holden was no longer business-suited but had changed and was now wearing a superbly tailored light-weight suit of pale grey.

Knowing absolutely nothing about his business, but accepting that perhaps in his league top executives always carried with them a change of less formal attire, Jazzlyn went forward. 'Something to drink, Jazzlyn?' he enquired, taking on the role of host since her father wasn't down yet.

'Something long and thirst-quenching,' she accepted, and spent a few minutes in general conversation with Holden and his aunt until Edwin Palmer joined them.

Quite when Jazzlyn began to pick up the sensation that all was not exactly as she had thought, she did not know. But, having adjourned to the dining room, they were midway through dinner when Mrs Williams brought in a bottle of white wine and asked Holden—as if *he* was host—if it was chilled enough. And later it was Holden whom she asked if everything was satisfactory.

'Splendid, as usual. Thank you, Mrs Williams,' he replied.

Well, he had been there before, Jazzlyn reasoned, and hadn't Mrs Williams greeted him as if she knew him when he'd first arrived? Having been able to find answers for the tiny questions that sprang to mind, she was just finishing off her meal when some sense of she knew not what—intuition, something in the air, whatever—made Jazzlyn suddenly again feel that there was something a little at odds.

'How long is it since you were here last?' Grace Craddock addressed her nephew, after she had mentioned to Edwin about a particularly fine painting Holden had in his London apartment.

'Friday, actually,' he replied.

Friday! Holden had been here last Friday! 'We arrived Saturday—we must have just missed you!' his aunt exclaimed.

'Must have.'

Jazzlyn began to feel a degree or two uncomfortable. She was here as Grace's guest, but to whom did Sandbanks belong—a friend of Grace, or a friend of Holden? Here Friday, here again today!

Jazzlyn found her voice. 'Do you come here to Sandbanks—er—fairly frequently?' she asked Holden direct.

It was her father who, on a teasing laugh, butted in before Holden could reply. 'Why wouldn't he, Jazzlyn? Didn't I mention that Holden owns Sandbanks?' And while Jazzlyn just sat there in stunned silence, her father added, 'Holden mainly spends the week at his London apartment, but otherwise he lives here. I thought you knew that!'

She wanted to die! Holden owned Sandbanks! It was his home! She was there as *Holden's* guest! Accepting *his* hospitality! Had in actual fact told him, 'You're welcome to stay with us', when all the while it was *his* home! Oh, the embarrassment of it! It was *unbearable*!

'I—er—didn't, actually,' she answered her parent, while at the same time wanting to be away from there as fast as she could. 'You've a very nice home.' Some courteous inner part of her voiced this polite opinion, but all she could manage was a flick of a glance to Holden.

Oh, hang it—she had noticed before, only that afternoon, that he saw too much, missed nothing, and she realised from the all-seeing grey-eyed stare that met her glance that Holden somehow knew a little of what she was feeling.

'It's my pleasure to be able to entertain friends and family here,' he replied quietly.

He had called her 'friend'. Had there been a faint emphasis on that word 'friends'? Was he saying it was a pleasure to entertain her? Jazzlyn was too het up to know. What she did know was that she had to get away, get out of there. But how?

Mrs Williams bringing in the coffee solved the problem. She thanked the housekeeper for the meal when the housekeeper enquired if she wanted more of anything. 'That was lovely, Mrs Williams. But I couldn't eat or drink another thing.' And then, when Mrs Williams had left the dining room, 'Would you excuse me?' Jazzlyn addressed no one in particular, and, hoping they would think she was about to take the dog for a walk, went as casually as she could manage from the dining room.

It had, she admitted, been in her mind to take Rembrandt for a walk in the cool of the evening, but somehow, finding that instead she had gone straight upstairs to her room, there was no way Jazzlyn intended going down again that night.

She felt a fool. Heavens, what a fool! 'You're welcome to stay with us', she'd told him. How crass! How big of her! He only owned the whole shot, that was all! So why had he asked her how she would feel about him staying on a few days? And, no wonder he'd taken on the role of host when he'd asked her if she'd like something to drink. He *was* host. It'd had nothing to do with her father not having been down yet.

Oh, why hadn't somebody *told* her? She was sure nobody had. Up until today, this evening, she hadn't picked up so much as a hint that Holden owned Sandbanks. Had he brought a change of clothes with him—he'd got a whole wardrobe here! Jazzlyn spent the rest of the evening going over the conversation she'd had with Grace and her father, but nowhere could she find a reference that the holiday home they were all enjoying belonged to Holden. On the face of it, Jazzlyn knew she had no cause to be upset. Holden had given a large hint that, as his friend, he was pleased to have her there. But that didn't make her feel any better.

She did not sleep well that night, and was awake very early, with the same thoughts pounding away in her head. Feeling mortified still that she could actually have told the house's owner that he was 'welcome to stay' with them, Jazzlyn leapt out of bed and went and took a shower.

Sensitive she might be, but anyone would be embarrassed under the circumstances, she thought unhappily as she donned underwear, shorts, a top and some sandals and silently left her room.

Rembrandt was there to greet her before she reached the bottom of the stairs. 'It's all right for you!' she told him. He wagged his tail cheerfully in response and she took them both off for a walk. No one else would be about at this hour, and, since he was unlikely to run off, she didn't bother hunting up his lead.

Rembrandt ran ahead and bounded back, full of joy on the deserted beach. She had been happy herself, prior to dinner last night,

Jazzlyn reflected. Oh, fancy telling him 'You're welcome to stay'!

Quite when she came to the conclusion that she was going to leave that day, she wasn't sure. But, having gone a considerable distance, she suddenly knew that it was the right thing to do.

She turned about. Even while somehow knowing in her heart that she didn't want to leave, pride, embarrassment, mortification—whatever it was—seemed to demand that to go back to Buckinghamshire was the only answer. Indeed, even Tony Johnstone and his pestering seemed to be the lesser of the two evils. Though why exactly that should be, she could not fathom.

Rembrandt, suddenly realising that she was going in the opposite direction, did a rapid turnaround and was soon with her again. Jazzlyn's thoughts were on her departure. Too bad she hadn't come in her own car. But, since she didn't want the smallest fuss, she'd get a taxi to the nearest railway station. Remmy was more than happy with Mrs Williams, and Mrs Williams seemed more than happy to have his company, so it would appear she wouldn't mind having him close by while Grace and her father took themselves off sketching.

With her mind made up, Jazzlyn speeded up her step. But, as she looked into the distance, suddenly she faltered. Someone was striding towards her, and he could only be coming from Sandbanks.

For male he certainly was, and it was not her father's gait. Rembrandt had seen him too, and took off at an enormous rate, greeting Holden rapturously. Jazzlyn speeded up again; she was embarrassed and didn't want to linger, to talk. Holden got nearer; her heartbeat went peculiar on her.

'Good morning!' she greeted him crisply. He was her host, she couldn't ignore him— though why she should want to confused her. She was about to speed on by, when Holden's hand snaked out and caught her by the arm, spinning her round to face him.

'Hey—what did I do?' he demanded, tall, long-legged—and, like her, in shorts.

She swallowed. 'Fickle hound!' was the best she could do.

'Me?' He seemed surprised—as well he might.

'Rembrandt,' she explained. The dog was still making an exuberant fuss of Holden.

'He's recognised me.'

'I didn't know the two of you were acquainted,' Jazzlyn commented coolly.

Holden eyed her sharply, not too enamoured of her cool tone, she could tell—well, he wouldn't have to put up with it for much longer. Soon she would be putting herself out of his orbit. But his tone was even when he revealed, 'We went for a long walk together last night.'

Make me feel guilty, why don't you! 'Thanks!' Jazzlyn mumbled—he could take Rembrandt for another long walk tonight. Her arm free, Holden having let it go, she went to march on.

'So—what did I do?' Holden repeated—a man not caring to have his questions unanswered, apparently.

Feeling more inclined to answer 'Nothing' than anything else, Jazzlyn's innate honesty chose that moment to trip her up. 'I'm leaving today,' she informed him solemnly.

'Because I've arrived?' Grey, uncompromising eyes stared into lovely violet ones. He was sharp, quick; she'd give him that.

'I didn't know you owned the house!' she said in a rush.

'You want me to apologise?'

She wanted to laugh. What *was* it about this man? Just a simple sentence, and he was straight through to her sense of humour.

'No, but…but you don't want all and sundry cluttering up your home.'

'You're fishing!' he accused.

'I'm leaving,' she answered, and no longer felt like laughing.

'I want you to stay,' he said, and made it sound as if he meant it. She shook her head. 'So I'm to be penalised because you're my guest and not my aunt's?' he challenged.

'Somebody should have—' Jazzlyn broke off, her eyes growing wide as she stared up at him. 'Penalised?' she queried.

'Look here, Jazzlyn Palmer…' Holden began severely. 'You and I have already established that we're pals, friends. That being so, I can relax with you, knowing that I don't have to concern myself that you might be plotting to get me to the altar.'

'Get you!' she scorned.

'Exactly,' he agreed. 'Sounds big-headed, I know, but I've sometimes had to take evasive action—as I know you have—so it's a tremendous relief to know I can enjoy your company without worrying you may have that tune of Mendelssohn's playing away in your head.'

He was referring to the 'Wedding March', of course. 'Heaven forbid!' she exclaimed tartly. But she owned that, what with Holden stating he wanted her to stay, and his hint that he enjoyed her company, she was starting to feel much less strung up about being his guest.

But she was staring at him wide-eyed again when he urged, 'Be kind to me, Jazzlyn. I need you here to protect me from my aunt's well-meaning efforts.'

'Grace?' she queried, startled once more.

'None other,' he confirmed. 'Dear to me though she is. Knowing that I'm taking a short holiday, nothing will give her greater pleasure than—if you're not here—to find me some female with whom I should make sandcastles.'

'You're not serious!' Jazzlyn exclaimed. He lived here most of the time and probably knew every female in the area. But... 'Oh!' she suddenly exclaimed, and then, at Holden's questioning look, 'Talking of sandcastles—I've a date down here tonight.'

He was not amused. 'Who with?' he demanded before she could blink.

'David Musgrove,' Jazzlyn answered, too taken aback by the sharply asked question to prevaricate.

'The GP?'

'The same. Your aunt introduced us.'

'See what I mean?' Holden drawled, his sharpness subsiding. 'My aunt has an incredible knack of—'

'She didn't purposely introduce us,' Jazzlyn butted in. 'We just sort of bumped into David when he was visiting a patient.' Holden didn't look convinced. 'I'd forgotten about him,' she went on to admit. 'I'd have remembered though, of course, before I went to catch my train.'

'You'd go—and leave me at my aunt's mercy?' Holden asked, with such charm that, against everything, Jazzlyn felt her defences start to crumble. 'I thought we were pals!' he reproached her.

'You—really want me to stay?' she questioned seriously. 'As your guest, I mean?' Her wide violet eyes stared into his.

Holden stared back, his eyes never leaving her face. Then he smiled, an utterly devastating smile. 'Who else do I know who'd come and have a swim in shorts and a top?' he asked.

Her heartbeat went wobbly. 'Swim?' she choked. Then, her voice gaining strength, 'You're suggesting I swim? Dressed as I am?'

His devastating smile became a devastating grin. 'I'll strip off if you will,' he offered.

She stared at him perhaps a few moments longer, then all at once the trauma and the tension of these past weeks disappeared entirely, and as a feeling of wonderful, carefree lightness spread all the way through her she held out her right hand. 'Pals,' she said, and experienced a tremendous feeling of light-hearted joy when Holden took her dainty hand in his and, his eyes on her face, shook hands on it.

'Pals,' he agreed.

He let go her hand, and Jazzlyn—suddenly giving in to a mad impulse—kicked off her sandals. 'What's keeping you?' she yelled, and hared off into the sea.

She took a header and, it being too early in the day for the sun to have made any impact on the water, came up with teeth chattering. She half turned—and spotted a similarly clad Holden swimming close by. Which one of them made the water first she had no idea, though suspected it was him.

'It's freezing!' she cried.

'Now aren't you glad you didn't take your clothes off?' he tormented, and she laughed— just had to. She had never felt so free, so at one with absolutely everything, so at peace within herself.

They didn't stay in the water very long; it was cold, and Holden was insisting that a jog back to Sandbanks would be more beneficial than staying in the water and turning a delicate shade of purple.

So together they jogged back to the house, Holden slowing his speed to hers, Rembrandt racing ahead. 'A hot shower,' Holden suggested as the dog disappeared in the direction of the kitchen and they stood in the hall prior to parting. Jazzlyn saw his eyes on her wet hair and glowing face. 'You truly are a most de-lightful female!' he added, every bit as if he couldn't help it.

'You're only saying that because I'm your only pal daft enough to take any notice of your ideas!' she jibed—a mite huskily, she had to own. 'I'm ruining your carpets!' she exclaimed as her soaked shorts started to drip—and with that she started hurriedly up the stairs.

'You're staying?' he called after her, stand-ing, not moving, where she had left him.

At the top of the stairs she turned and dropped him a little curtsey. 'Thank you for asking—I'd love to,' she answered.

Unspeaking, Holden nodded, then walked out of her line of vision, and Jazzlyn turned and hurried on to her room. But it was only after a hot shower, when she had shampooed her hair and was blow drying it, that she no-ticed in the bathroom mirror the look of hap-piness in her eyes. It was then that Jazzlyn felt the first stirrings of doubt about her friendship with Holden Hathaway.

She had been happy talking with him. Supremely, light-heartedly happy with him when, without bothering to change into a swimsuit, she had swum with him. She had been laughing with him as she'd jogged back with him. But was it natural to be this happy to be with someone who was just a friend?

She had other friends she spent time with, but couldn't remember ever feeling the same inner glow with them that she'd felt when she'd been with Holden. It could, she supposed, be purely and simply the result of letting go on the knotted-up tension caused by Tony Johnstone's phone calls. But somehow she was very unsure. She'd been happy before without being aware she was happy. Now, with Holden, she felt happy and—as if everything was heightened when he was around—she *was* aware she was happy. It made her wary.

The household was only now starting to stir. Jazzlyn stayed in her room. Some instinct was deciding for her that it might be a good idea—since she had accepted to stay—if she kept out of Holden's way as much as possible.

That, she later discovered, was exceptionally easy to achieve. Because, on hearing her father leave his room, she went down to join everyone for breakfast. She found that Grace and her nephew were already in the breakfast room, and were discussing going into town.

'Holden's driving me to the shops,' Grace told Edwin Palmer. 'You don't want to come, do you?'

'Not unless you think I should,' he answered diplomatically.

'Didn't think you did.' Grace smiled. 'Jazzlyn?'

'I thought I'd do some sketching,' Jazzlyn answered.

'Want anything bringing back?' Holden asked easily, plainly not bothered one way or the other if she went with them or not.

'No thanks,' she replied—and after they'd gone, helping herself to a large sun umbrella on the way out, she took herself off, wondering what in creation was the matter with her. She was sure she didn't give a button that, in the manner of companionable friendship, Holden would have been quite happy had she said she'd like to go with them, but was equally happy that he was not to have the pleasure of her company.

And what about her own 'happy' feelings? She had been happy earlier. Still was, she supposed, yet—something was niggling away at her. She set up camp in the sand dunes and shrugged away the faint sensation of feeling a touch peeved—she must be growing moody in her old age.

She was still there some hours later, musing on the possibility of cancelling her date with David Musgrove, when, getting up and glancing towards the beach, she caught a distant glimpse of her father and Grace walking hand in hand along the shoreline. They were back, then, Grace and Holden.

Experiencing something ridiculously like disquiet that Holden so wanted her friendship during his short break that he couldn't be bothered to come and look for her, Jazzlyn pulled herself up short. Grief! As if she cared! To blazes with cancelling her date with David Musgrove. She'd go, and have a jolly good time.

Not that the fact of her going out on a date that night bothered her 'friend' in any way, she discovered. And perish the thought that she might want it to! She most definitely didn't. Realising that her experience with Tony Johnstone must have unsettled her more than had been apparent, Jazzlyn, out of courtesy to Mrs Williams returned to the house at lunch-time.

Having been up to her room to tidy herself, prior to a light lunch, she found everyone was in the dining room when she went in. 'Am I late? Sorry!' she apologised.

'You're not late,' Grace smiled. 'We're early.'

'Have a good shop?' Jazzlyn asked, taking her place at the table.

'Have a good sketch?' Holden butted in to ask.

Jazzlyn looked at him, affable, friendly, good-looking. 'I'm hopeless at it,' she owned.

'You can't be good at everything,' he answered lightly.

She wanted to laugh. 'True,' she agreed, and did laugh—and wondered why her heart gave a little flutter when Holden grinned.

The moment was over, for the next instant he was addressing some remark to his aunt, but Jazzlyn felt strangely warmed by that sharing moment.

'You're not eating very much,' Grace commented of the small amount of smoked salmon and salad on her plate. Then, remembering, she said, 'You must be saving your appetite for dinner with David Musgrove tonight.'

Jazzlyn smiled at her, but before she could find any sort of reply Holden revealed how *un*-bothered he was by offering, in friendly fashion, 'I'm going out myself early this evening. I'll give you a lift if you like!'

Where was *he* going? A date, obviously. 'David's calling for me. Thanks all the same,' she smiled, and munched her way through her salad somehow. As Grace had observed, she didn't seem to have much of an appetite this lunchtime.

Holden spent the afternoon in his study, and was still nowhere about when Jazzlyn answered the door to David Musgrove. She was ready, but invited him in to introduce him to her father. 'Have a good time,' Grace bade them when a few minutes later they left.

'How's the holiday going?' David asked as they drove along.

'Wonderfully relaxing,' she replied.

'Have you been swimming yet?'

'I went swimming this morning,' she answered, and just had to smile at the memory.

David was a very pleasant man to go out with, but Jazzlyn knew before she'd finished her soup that never, should it rain pig's pudding, would he ever invite her to swim dressed as she was.

It seemed impolite to think of Holden when she was out with someone else, and Jazzlyn made herself give David her full attention. Only it wasn't that easy, because time and again she found that she was having to pull her thoughts back from the owner of Sandbanks.

She glanced around the restaurant, as if expecting that he might have chosen the same one to dine in. It was a certainty that he was dining out this evening. So why, she wondered—a shade miffed, she had to own—did he need a friend around? All he had to do was to tell his aunt that he was seeing somebody, and Grace would put away her penchant for introducing him to unattached women.

Still, she supposed, given she was spending a fortnight holidaying in his home, the least she could do in return was to be his unmatrimonially-minded pal.

Again she ousted Holden from her thoughts. 'Given that your work must be unbearably stressed at times, do you enjoy being a doctor?' she asked David—and made every effort to give him all her attention as he told her a little of his work.

They had finished eating by ten-thirty. But when David suggested they walk around for a little while Jazzlyn declined. She liked David well enough, but she was ready to go back to Sandbanks.

'Do you mind if we don't? I want to be up early tomorrow to take the dog for a walk before it gets too hot,' she invented on the spot, and so committed herself to get up with the birds.

There were various lights on in the house when, a little after eleven, they arrived back at Sandbanks. David got out of the car with her, and while it had been in Jazzlyn's mind to thank him for a very pleasant evening and bid him goodnight—she didn't get the chance. Because even as she opened her mouth to get started, so, out of nowhere it seemed, Holden, with Rembrandt in tow, suddenly appeared.

'Hello, David,' he greeted her escort affably, coming forward to shake his hand. As Jazzlyn bent to make a fuss of the dog, he invited, 'Coming in for a cup of coffee?'

'Love one,' David accepted. And Jazzlyn was left feeling little short of thunderstruck—okay, it was Holden's house, but it was *her* place to invite, or not, her escort for an end-of-the-evening coffee.

'Where did you eat?' Holden asked her conversationally as the three of them went indoors.

Where did you? 'A super little place!' she enthused. 'The Old Shilling.'

She found that Holden, while explaining that Mrs Williams was off duty, was ushering them into the kitchen. More, found that she had been appointed coffee-maker-in-chief! What were friends for? She set about making three cups of coffee while the two men discussed the merits and non-merits of the various eating establishments within a fifteen-mile radius of the village of Havorton.

'Coffee,' she smiled, sitting down at the kitchen table—where the fickle Rembrandt had changed his affections again to appear besotted with Holden. The conversation, she realised, had now moved on to things engineering in the medical line.

Five minutes later, and totally fed up with men and dog, Jazzlyn had had enough. She went to the sink and rinsed her cup and saucer, and was ready when the tiniest pause appeared in the conversation.

'If no one minds, I think I'll go to bed,' she jumped in sweetly.

Both men were instantly on their feet. 'Must you go yet?' David asked, clearly believing he had been chatting to Holden for mere seconds, not minutes.

'Thank you for a lovely evening,' she trotted out, putting some space between them lest he thought she might be seeking the reward of a kiss to her cheek. 'Er—Holden...' She addressed him without looking at him—he'd invited David in; let him entertain him. 'I—um—shouldn't like Mrs Williams to be greeted by the sight of dirty dishes in the morning.'

She looked at Holden then, but could tell nothing of how he was taking being more or less ordered to wash up in his own home.

Though, could she not tell? If she wasn't very much mistaken, there was nothing but laughter dancing in those fine grey eyes.

'Neither would I,' he agreed pleasantly.

'Goodnight!' she said collectively, and hurriedly left the room. To the blazes with the pair of them. Jazzlyn ran swiftly up the stairs and owned that, after quite an enjoyable evening, she was feeling very much out of sorts.

CHAPTER FOUR

EVEN without her guilt-salving commitment to get up early the next day, Jazzlyn was awake at first light. She had not slept well and saw no point in lingering in bed. After a quick shower, she dressed in jeans and a white tee shirt and went looking for Rembrandt.

He thumped his tail vigorously when he saw her. 'Come on, then,' she called in hushed tones, and he needed no more of an invitation than that.

Jazzlyn took the same route she had taken the previous morning, but this time on her return journey she saw neither hide nor hair of Holden. Not that she wanted to. It seemed incredible to her now that twenty-four hours ago she, at his instigation, had run into the sea totally and absolutely uncaring of how she was dressed!

Her lips twitched. She straightened them. She didn't want her sense of humour reasserting itself. It was funny, though. As it was funny—if she cared to see the funny side of it—the way she had left David with Holden, chatting over the coffee cups. Then she recalled how Holden had been back from his date before her last night. And had, by the look of it, been taking Remmy for a walk when she had come home. So, on that evidence, his date couldn't have been all that 'heavy'.

Having slept badly, and not being in the most sunny of moods when she'd left the house, Jazzlyn felt in much better spirits when she got back to Sandbanks. The walk, she realised as she entered the house, had done her a power of good.

Rembrandt took off, bounding up to Holden, who was just coming down the stairs. 'You want to get up in the morning!' said she—who had been up over an hour.

'It's my blameless conscience!' he decreed—a teasing hint there that her guilty conscience kept her awake. 'Give me a call tomorrow morning,' he suggested as they met at the bottom of the stairs. 'Unless you prefer your own company?'

'It's the swimwear I'm not so keen on,' she laughed, and headed up the stairs. It looked like being another glorious day.

Rembrandt went to make up to Mrs Williams after breakfast, and while Edwin Palmer and Grace took off in the Range Rover, and Holden went with the morning's mail to his study, Jazzlyn went to offer her services to Mrs Williams. But she found that Nancy from the village had already arrived, and that her help was not needed. Jazzlyn went up to her room, changed into a cropped top and shorts, and then, with paperback and sketching materials in hand, and collecting the sun umbrella on the way, she left the house and made for what was fast becoming her favourite place.

She settled herself down, but her sketchpad remained blank. She took up her paperback, a thriller, but found she was reading the same paragraph over and over again. She didn't know how long Holden was here, or how long he was able to take off work, but she was glad he was taking a break—albeit that at this very moment he was working in his study.

As the sun moved round she got up to adjust her sunshade. She contemplated going back to the house for a swimsuit and taking a swim. She resisted the idea and settled down with her book again. Ten minutes later she felt her heartbeat suddenly quicken when, out of nowhere, Holden unexpectedly appeared. He had a car rug in one hand, a bottle of lemonade and a couple of glasses in the other.

'Who gave you permission to leave your study?' she asked, finding she was feeling strangely tongue-tied and in need of something to say.

'I was at my bedroom window when I thought I spotted a thirsty damsel up here. What are you reading?'

Jazzlyn showed him the cover of her book. 'It's riveting,' said she, who'd barely turned over three pages in the past forty-five minutes.

'I've read it,' Holden informed her. 'I was certain the superintendent did it, but it was—'

'Don't you dare!'

Holden grinned, and Jazzlyn realised that he hadn't been going to tell her who the murderer was anyway. 'You're covered in sand. Stand up,' he instructed.

Bossy brute! She liked him, and got to her feet. Jazzlyn waited until he had spread the car rug, then took her ease again. Holden poured her a glass of lemonade, handed it to her, poured himself a glass, then joined her on the rug.

'Musgrove rang,' he thought to mention.

'For me?'

'I told him to ring back. Are you going out with him again?'

She thought Holden was the nosiest male friend she had. 'You don't think I should wait until I'm asked?'

'He'll ask.'

He sounded sure of it. 'I'll wait until then.'

'That'll be two out of three,' Holden reminded her conversationally, and she recalled having more or less told him that—Tony the exception—she seldom dated anyone more than three times.

'I'm only here for a fortnight!' she laughed. A seagull chose that moment to glide overhead, so they fell into an inconsequential discussion on seagulls.

In fact, over the next few days it seemed to her that they discussed almost every subject under the sun. It was Saturday before she knew it, and she and Holden had taken to swimming together every afternoon. She hadn't had to give him a call when she'd taken Rembrandt for his early-morning walk on Thursday. Holden, with Rembrandt beside him, had been up, dressed and sitting in an antique chair on the landing waiting for her as she'd quietly left her room. Her heart had lifted.

'You'll get shot!' she'd whispered—Rembrandt was definitely not allowed upstairs. Holden had affected extreme innocence.

Her heart had lifted yesterday morning too when, before the rest of the house was on the move, she, Holden and the dog had been out on the beach. When Holden hadn't been throwing sticks for Rembrandt he'd been asking her about her work, her play, her hobbies. In fact such general chat that might pass between any two new friends who were learning about each other, with nothing in any of their conversations that would lead to them being more than that.

Jazzlyn felt totally relaxed with Holden. Relaxed and entirely unthreatened. For her part she grew to feel that she could discuss positively anything with him, and mainly she did. She asked him about his work, his travel—but, above all she wanted to know who his girl-friend was of Tuesday night, she could not ask.

She looked out of her bedroom window early that Saturday morning and saw it looked like the start of another beautiful sun-filled day. David had phoned yesterday, wanting to take her out, but she had put him off. He was on duty this weekend, so she reckoned he wouldn't contact her again before Monday, when, possibly, she might feel more like going out with him again.

Jazzlyn wasted no more time. She was on holiday, she was free—and the weather was terrific. What was she waiting for? In next to no time she was showered and dressed and si-lently leaving her room.

She was a trifle disappointed that Holden wasn't sitting there in the same spot he had been on Thursday and Friday morning. But with a quick stretch over the landing rail she saw that he and Rembrandt were downstairs waiting.

They seemed to tramp miles that morning, throwing sticks, pausing, talking, stepping it out. And it was all too much. 'Isn't this just too, too, blissful!' Jazzlyn sighed, in complete harmony with absolutely everything around her.

'Enjoying your holiday?'

'Doesn't it show?' she asked, and was surprised when Holden halted. As she halted too, he looked down into her face.

'You certainly seem a lot less wound up than you were when you came here,' he commented seriously.

She didn't want him serious. He was her pal. He made her laugh. And, while she was aware that they were both referring to the effect Tony Johnstone's stalking had had on her, Tony could be a million miles away as far as she was concerned. She certainly didn't want to be reminded of him.

'Totally unwound, I'd say,' she answered brightly.

Holden continued to scrutinise her face, his eyes resting on her clear, unclouded violet eyes, then moving to her sweetly curving lips, to her chin and dainty features.

'Promise me something?' he asked.

He seemed even more serious. She didn't want him more serious. But it seemed he was not ready to move on until she had given him her promise. 'If I can,' she replied.

'Promise that if, when you get back home, this Tony phones, or contacts you by any means—or if he's waiting for you when you leave anywhere—you'll contact me and let me deal with it.'

She was taken back. 'Not my father?' she asked, startled.

'From what's happened so far, I'd say you'd put up with more weeks of harassment before you told your father.' Jazzlyn realised he was probably right. She felt so much more able to cope now than she had when she'd come away. How long, though, would it take for Tony to wear her down again?

'I don't think he'll ring again. I truly don't,' she said softly. How kind Holden was.

'Promise me!' he insisted.

'But...' she began to protest. It was her problem, not his.

'Promise!' He was immovable. But he was also her friend.

'I promise,' she gave in, and, purely because she seemed unable to do anything else, stretched up and placed a grateful kiss on his cheek. 'Oh!' she exclaimed. 'Is that allowed between friends?'

For long, long moments Holden stood silently, staring down at her. And suddenly she had the oddest notion that he was going to return the compliment and kiss her. But he did not. Instead he switched his gaze out to sea, over her shoulder, and then, his serious look fading, informed her, 'I'll make an exception in your case. But don't make a habit of it.'

She had to grin, and they fell into step once more. The sauce of it—he had once kissed her cheek as a thank you, she recalled. Cheek-kissing wasn't his sole right, she reflected cheerfully.

Back at the house they went their separate ways, with Jazzlyn going to her room for a quick wash and tidy up before joining the others for the first meal of the day. She entered the breakfast room, not knowing why her eyes should glance to see if Holden was there. He looked her way in friendly fashion.

'Good morning,' she offered generally, and discovered she had come in in the middle of a discussion on supermarket shopping. Apparently Grace had drawn up a list of requirements with Mrs Williams, and had said she would do the shopping. 'My father loves supermarkets,' Jazzlyn teased; come to think of it, her father hated shopping of any kind!

'For you, Grace, I'd willingly forfeit a planned morning's sketching.' Edwin Palmer spoke up gallantly, blanching a little, it was true.

'No need,' Holden joined in—and had three pairs of eyes fixed on him when he volunteered, 'I'll go!'

'You can't!' his aunt protested in astonishment. 'You'll bring back all the wrong things!'

Jazzlyn was sure that Grace was right, though she realised that after the hard work and tough decisions he must take daily in his work to wheel a trolley around a supermarket would be a holiday in itself for him. She was unsure, though, for whose benefit it was—his, or his aunt's, who was sure he'd make a hash of it—that she found herself piping up, 'I'll go with you if you like.'

Her offer was instantly taken up. 'I thought you'd never bite,' Holden accepted dryly.

In an attempt to be there before the supermarket got too crowded, they decided to go as soon as breakfast was over. Seated beside Holden in his car as they headed out of the village towards the nearest town, Jazzlyn started to realise just how content she felt. Perhaps a leisurely trundle around a supermarket was part and parcel of her relaxing break too. She owned that, though she had travelled to more exotic places, her present holiday ranked as the best she'd ever had.

She fell to wondering if Holden was enjoying his break too, and then, with a start, realised that he would more than likely be going back to work on Monday. He'd said last Monday that he was taking a few days off but, given that he spent quite a bit of his time in his study working, that 'few days' had stretched into four.

'Are you going back to London on Monday?' she asked abruptly, suddenly finding that she needed to know.

'What brought that on?' he asked easily.

'You said you were only having a few days off!' she reminded him.

'Crack the whip, why don't you!'

She smiled. 'I think I shall probably miss you,' Jazzlyn told him in her open way.

'I've enjoyed your company too' Holden replied. He pulled into the car park of the supermarket and searched for a free space. 'Have you got the list?' he asked matter-of-factly.

'You had it,' she told him. Men!

Somehow she felt a touch niggled. 'I've enjoyed your company too' he'd said—he could have been asking her to pass the cruet for all his comment had sounded like a compliment. For pity's sake, why would he compliment her about anything? They were friends and nothing more—why would she seek compliments? Banish such thoughts.

Jazzlyn's good humour was soon restored when she saw the hash he was making of shopping. 'Who looks after you in London?' she just had to ask, taking several tins of peaches that weren't on the list out of the trolley and putting them back on the shelves.

'I look after myself!' he defied her to argue, though he did concede, 'I have been known to eat the occasional meal out.'

'Only occasional?' She didn't believe it.

'Are you going to report me to my aunt?'

'Not if you behave yourself.' She was happy; she owned up to it. When she saw a most delectable little toddler in the child seat of a trolley, she just couldn't resist a friendly, 'Hello, sweetheart.'

'You like children?' Holden asked conversationally as they moved on.

'Doesn't everyone?' she asked absently, pausing to study Grace's list.

'Yet—you've decided never to get married,' he remarked, and caused Jazzlyn to forget her list and to raise her head and stare at him. His expression was unsmiling, his question serious, she realised. The supermarket was crowded, but somehow Holden had pushed their trolley into an isolated spot between the delicatessen and the cooked meats counters.

She decided to give him a serious answer. 'I'm perfectly aware that it's not essential to be married in order to have a child. But so far I've never met a man whom I would wish to be the father of my child.' That, she felt, nicely put the subject away. Now to get on with the shopping.

But even as she went to move on Holden was taking it further, when, still in that same easy conversational way he had, he commented, 'Which means you must be taking every precaution to prevent yourself from becoming pregnant.'

She stopped dead in her tracks, her lovely violet eyes shooting wide in astonishment. Okay, he was her friend—but were they *really* having this discussion about her sex-life between the cooked meats and the coleslaw sections?

'I only need one precaution,' she erupted shortly. She could tell that she had his complete attention—his eyes never left her face. But, not putting it past him to ask what that precaution was, she went on before he could ask. 'I use the word ''No'',' she told him coolly. And was pleased that she seemed to have startled him for a change.

He was staring at her as if hardly believing what he'd heard. He was obviously totally oblivious to their surroundings when he questioned, 'Always?' She refused to answer, but found she was somehow hemmed in by him, a wall, and a three-quarters-full trolley when, rocking back slightly on his heels, he asked, 'Er—sweet Jazzlyn, do I take it you've never—um—said yes?'

Her right hand itched. She wanted to box his ears. But she knew that they were in a su- permarket, even if he seemed to have forgot- ten. 'Some do—I *don't*!' she told him snap- pily, and could have crowned him when, suddenly, he was grinning from ear to ear.

'You sweet old-fashioned thing, you,' he said softly.

'You're asking for a black eye!' she hissed pugilistically.

He stopped grinning, stared at her mouth— and, taking charge of the trolley again, said, 'Bacon,' and left her to trail after him.

Pig! She didn't want to be his friend any more. He'd laughed at her when—and only at his insistence—she had revealed that she was a virgin. She toyed with the idea of leaving him at the checkout to pack everything away by himself. Knowing him, though, half a dozen eager-to-please assistants would be there to do the job for him.

Jazzlyn was not feeling any more amiable towards him when they eventually reached that destination. A streak of fairness in her—which she really did not want—would not be denied, though, and she was right there with him, loading and packing—and getting her credit card out to pay. Only to be made more annoyed when he pushed it back at her and insisted on paying himself.

'The toothpaste is mine. It's not on Grace's list,' she told him belligerently.

'Allow me to pay for it so I may see the shine of your lovely smile,' he answered, and while the woman on the till positively beamed to hear such charm, Jazzlyn was hard put to it not to bare her teeth at him.

Unfortunately, though, she could feel her sense of humour resurfacing as they trundled the laden trolley back to the car. She didn't want to be charmed by him; she didn't. But, she admitted, he was seriously getting to her.

The shopping had been stowed, trolley housed, and they were both sitting in his car when, instead of starting the engine, Holden turned in his seat. 'Still mad at me?' he asked.

She turned her head to look at him. 'The next time you fancy a discussion on my sex-life—or lack of it—perhaps you wouldn't mind choosing somewhere other than a crowded supermarket on a Saturday morning,' she replied, as sternly as she could manage.

'Now there's an invitation!' he countered. But his expression was wholly serious when he asked, 'Going to forgive me, Jazzlyn?'

Who could resist? She liked him so well. 'You knew I would.'

He looked at her for a few moments more, then, to set her heartbeats thundering, his head started to come nearer. She thought he was aiming for her mouth, but, knowing that she should move, she felt strangely too mesmer-ised to take evasive action. Then she discov-ered that evasive action wasn't needed. For his kiss, his gentle kiss, landed not on her lips but on her cheek.

'Now who's making a habit of it?' she chal-lenged as he pulled back and started the car's engine. But her voice was husky and not at all like her own. This friend of hers, she realised, was having the oddest effect on her.

They journeyed back in companionable si-lence and, having arrived at Sandbanks, drove around to the rear where Jazzlyn was surprised to see the Range Rover.

'I thought they'd have gone sketching ages ago!' she exclaimed, going to the rear of Holden's car to help him carry in the shopping.

They didn't get to lift more than one bag, however, before Grace appeared, followed by Jazzlyn's father. 'Archie's ill,' Grace said without preamble. 'We were just on our way out when his neighbour phoned.' Archie, Jazzlyn remembered, was Grace's philandering ex-husband. Archie—who got in touch when he was in trouble.

While Jazzlyn looked to her father, Holden, she realised, had taken in what his aunt had said, and was adding it to what he knew of her. 'I'll take you,' he said at once, seeming to know she would feel she had to go to aid her ex-husband.

'It's already arranged,' Edwin Palmer stated, 'I'm taking Grace.' And Jazzlyn could see that Holden's respect for her father went up a notch because, for Grace's sake, Edwin was prepared to put aside his aversion to having anything to do with the man who had caused her so many years of unhappiness. 'We only waited for you to get back,' Edwin went on, and, turning to his daughter, he continued, 'I'm not sure what situation we'll find—but I'll take Remmy with me.' And in the following five minutes, with Grace saying she would ring as soon as they got there, to let them know what the situation was, Edwin Palmer and Grace were on their way.

'How do you feel about melted ice cream?' Holden asked as the Range Rover disappeared around the corner.

'Oh, grief!' Jazzlyn exclaimed, having forgotten every bit about the shopping. They spent the next half an hour bringing the bags in and putting their purchases away—clearly Holden had little idea, domestically, of what went where.

'Coffee?' Holden suggested when they were finished.

'I'll make it,' she offered, and he let her. He was good at that, she recalled. 'Shall I make Mrs Williams one?' Jazzlyn asked, not having seen the housekeeper since their return, but not wanting to leave her out of a coffee break.

'She's not here—she's at her sister's. I've given her the weekend off.'

'Oh, that's good!' Jazzlyn said spontaneously. 'Oh, I don't mean good because—'

'I know what you mean,' Holden interrupted softly. 'You mean good because after looking after us all this week she deserves a break.'

'You're getting to know me.'

Holden looked at her for long and—she felt—sensitive seconds. 'I rather think I am. You're a very lovely person, Jazzlyn,' he added quietly.

Her breath seemed caught in the middle of her throat somewhere. She realised that she wanted him to think well of her—and wondered why that surprised her. Everybody wanted to be thought well of, didn't they? So why, particularly, did she want Holden's good opinion?

He was having some effect on her, she knew that, but conversely she fought to deny it. 'If you're fishing for me to return the compliment, forget it,' she found out of a confused nowhere. 'And you're still cooking dinner tonight!'

Holden laughed, and looked wonderful. She never wanted him to be cross with her. But suddenly, as his laughter faded, she sensed a kind of tension in the air. He was staring at her, seemed to be taking in every detail of her face. Then she blinked, and it was all in her head, she realised, for Holden was just the same as he always was—off hand, almost, as he reached for the coffee she had just poured him and told her, 'I'll take mine in the study.'

Friends. Pals. Jazzlyn found she was having to make herself remember that when in all honesty she had to admit she was feeling a smidgen out of sorts that Holden clearly preferred to drink his coffee in the solitude of his study than in company with her. Friends could do that sort of thing; it didn't mean anything. And hadn't he just said he thought her a lovely person? For goodness' sake, she'd got nothing in the world to feel miffed about.

Anyway, Holden always spent a good part of the morning at work in his study. So, okay, today was Saturday, but she doubted very much that he had got to be on the board of Zortek International by working purely Monday to Friday.

Having satisfactorily concluded that it meant nothing personal that Holden, having taken a couple of hours out of his day to do the supermarket shopping, was now busily catching up, Jazzlyn decided she would take a stroll along the beach. Her father and Grace wouldn't have reached their destination yet, but Holden would be home in the event of there being any phone calls.

Jazzlyn did not walk very far. She was feeling fidgety, restless, and somehow not at peace with herself. She retraced her steps and entered the kitchen. She popped some half-baked baguettes in the oven to crisp up, and began to prepare a salad for lunch. She found she was feeling better for being busy.

'Something smells good!'

She hadn't heard Holden coming, and jumped when she looked up and saw him in the doorway. 'Don't get your hopes up. It's only bread,' she told him, knowing that she would probably be the one to cook dinner, but not ready yet to let him into that little secret.

'Want a hand?'

'Almost finished,' she refused.

'Shall we eat here?'

'Why not?'

Jazzlyn munched her way through her salad and appreciated Holden's company. Together they loaded the dishwasher and tidied up, and she was glad that her equilibrium had returned.

'Going back to your study?' she enquired, thinking of the couple of hours he had missed by doing the shopping.

'I've told you before about cracking that whip' he reminded her, and then the phone rang. He took the call on the kitchen phone. Had it been personal for him she would have taken herself off somewhere. But her guess that it was Grace proved a correct one. 'Hire a nurse,' she heard Holden say. 'Well, don't wear yourself out. You know you owe him nothing.' By the sound of it, the philandering Archie was ill enough to need professional assistance. 'Jazzlyn's right here. I'll put her on.'

Holden handed the phone to her. Their fingers touched, and Jazzlyn felt a tingle shoot through her. Good heavens! 'Hello, Grace,' she said, getting herself under control. 'How are things?'

'The doctor's been. Archie has a severe bout of flu.'

'Oh, I'm sorry.' Flu, she knew, especially in someone of mature years, could be quite a serious illness.

'So am I! Archie was never a very good patient at the best of times. However, I can't leave him like this, on his own.'

'Of course not.' He didn't deserve that anyone as good as Grace should look after him, but Jazzlyn well knew that Grace wasn't the type of person who could so easily walk away. 'My father...' she began.

'He's a gem,' Grace said softly. 'I never fully appreciated that until now. He's very good in a sickroom—and Archie's hating it. Would you like to speak to your father?' Before Jazzlyn could answer, she went on, 'I'll go and give him a call; he's helping Archie into some clean pyjamas.'

A silence followed, then Edwin Palmer was picking up the phone. 'Are you all right, Jazzlyn?' he asked.

'I'm fine. It's you I'm more concerned about.'

'Don't be. We've lost our holiday, by the look of it, but that can't be helped. Grace being the kind person she is wouldn't be able to live with the guilt if she left Craddock to his own miserable devices.'

'No, I'm—' Jazzlyn broke off, a fresh implication hitting her. 'Are you saying that you won't be coming back?'

'It's very unlikely. Flu, if you remember when I had it, goes on for weeks and weeks. Will you be able to make it back home under your own steam? Perhaps Holden will give you a lift back.'

'You've got enough to worry about there,' Jazzlyn told him brightly, and came away from the phone knowing that her holiday, too, was over—and she did not want it to be. 'My father's helping out with the nursing,' she offered, suddenly realising that Holden had been standing there watching her all this while.

'So Grace said,' he replied; and astute wasn't the word for it, 'Why so pensive?'

'No wonder you're on the board of Zortek!'

'I'm sure there's a compliment in there somewhere,' Holden replied good-humouredly, but, tenacious to the end, he persisted, 'What's bothering you, Jazzlyn?'

He was going to have to know anyway. 'I think it's best all round if I go home,' she answered, and was about to say what a lovely time she'd had when she noticed that all sign of good humour had gone from him.

'I thought we'd already had this conversation!' he said sharply.

'Well, pardon me for bringing it up again!' she retorted snappily.

'You're unhappy here?' he questioned curtly.

'You know I'm not!'

'I've offended you in some way?' he demanded.

And Jazzlyn's spurt of temper abruptly fizzled out. 'You know you haven't,' she answered softly.

'So why punish me?'

'*Punish* you!' She stared at him incredulously.

'Punish,' he confirmed, and went on, 'I mentioned only this morning how less wound up you are now—have you no idea how relaxing it is for *me*, to have a break in uncomplicated female company?'

Jazzlyn, perversely, wasn't sure that she appreciated 'uncomplicated', but it made her feel good, she couldn't deny, that this break was doing Holden as much good as it was doing her—and that, by his intimation, she had played a small part in it.

'You—want me to stay on?' she asked.

Holden nodded, studying her, watching her before, his manner easy, relaxed, he asked, 'Who's going to eat all that food we bought this morning? More to the point, if you go— who's going to cook it?'

She grinned; she had to. She knew full well that she was being weak, that she was only here anyway because Grace was his aunt. But, when it came to the final analysis, she knew that truly she just did not want to leave.

CHAPTER FIVE

HOLDEN, as Jazzlyn had fully anticipated, barely knew how to light a gas jet, it seemed, much less how to cook on one. She had taken herself off for a stroll around the village that afternoon, and had taken in a paddle along the beach on the way home. But it was at around half past six, after taking a shower and donning some fresh white trousers and a shirt, that she was on her way to the kitchen when she came across Holden, who was coming to look for her.

'Is there anything I should be doing, do you suppose?' he asked, winning charm there in every syllable, and Jazzlyn couldn't help but smile.

'There speaks a man who's just experienced the first sensation that something to eat around half past seven might prove a problem.'

He looked at her solemnly, then his expression fractured into a grin which Jazzlyn was sure must have devastated many women. She owned she felt a little feeble in the region of her heart herself.

'Go on, Jazz,' he coaxed, and she couldn't help it—she burst out laughing.

'Come with me,' she ordered. 'I'll teach you how to scrape new potatoes.'

To her surprise, she found him a willing pupil, but because of his slowness with the unfamiliar task, and because she wanted to set the potatoes to boil before she did anything else, she found another knife and joined him at the sink.

Then she wondered if that was such a good idea. Their hands met in the water and she pulled jerkily back, feeling disturbed somehow. He looked down at her, his glance seeming to look into her very soul, unsmiling, serious, sensitive, as if trying to fathom what had startled her.

Jazzlyn looked away from him, ran the tap and rinsed her hands. 'This sink's not big enough for both of us!' she told him shortly, and, as she got her second wind, she decided, 'Anyhow, you're big enough to do this job on your own.'

'Bossy baggage!' he accused pleasantly, and Jazzlyn left him to go and get a couple of steaks out of the fridge.

By the time they were eating Jazzlyn had got herself back together again, and was ready to scorn entirely any notion that Holden disturbed her in any way. He, she noted, was exactly the same as he ever was—good company, able to chat about absolutely anything, easy to get along with. In fact—a friend.

So why, once she'd left him and was up in her room, did she start to feel restless? It was almost as if, having parted from him for the evening, she wanted to be back with him again. Good grief! The sunny weather must be going to her head!

Having scoffed at such ridiculous and far-flung notions, Jazzlyn was up early the next morning and, even with Rembrandt not there, saw no reason to deny herself the enjoyment of a pre-breakfast walk along the beach.

She owned to feeling quite pleased to have company when she saw Holden waiting for her downstairs. 'Decided to have your constitutional before it gets too hot?' he enquired as they fell into step.

'Do you often walk this early when you're not having a break from work?' she asked him.

'Always,' he replied. 'Especially on a Sunday.' The trouble with holidays was that one tended to forget what day of the week it was. Today was Sunday, she realised. Though he was teasing, and lying about always taking an early-morning walk—she was sure of it.

'Fibber!' she accused.

'But never with such a superb companion!' he said gallantly, as if she hadn't spoken.

'Lay it on with a trowel!' she jibed, and he laughed, his expression on her gentle.

Jazzlyn had an inner feeling that Holden had been as happy as she had on that walk. She returned to her room when they got back to Sandbanks, and after changing her shoes went downstairs to the kitchen with the intention of making them both some breakfast. She discovered that he knew quite well how to work a toaster. The kitchen table was laid, and breakfast was all ready for her!

'Poached eggs on toast all right, madam?' he asked, draining an egg for her prior to setting it down on buttered toast.

'Thank you, my man,' she said loftily, and as she looked at him saw a spasm of something she just could not interpret cross his expression a moment before he turned from her. 'Er—is Mrs Williams coming back this evening?' she asked.

He shook his head. 'I'm picking her up from the station tomorrow morning.'

Tomorrow was Monday. 'You're not going to work?' she asked, surprised.

'I'm due some time off,' he answered, and before she had a chance to think about that he offered, 'We could go out to dinner tonight if you don't fancy cooking.'

'You think I'd let you off kitchen duties so easily?' she questioned.

An hour later, dressed in a bikini top and shorts, having taken the rug and sunshade off to the sand dunes while Holden closeted himself in his study, Jazzlyn questioned herself as to why she had turned down his offer of dinner out. Was she being perverse, or what? She would quite like to dine out with him, so why had she declined? She began to feel fidgety and restless again, but just could not fathom what was getting to her. It wasn't a date as such, for goodness' sake—and in any case friends didn't have 'dates', did they? It was more an expediency. One of them—i.e. her—was going to have to cook. Holden was merely attempting to save her the bother.

Jazzlyn went back to the house to don a skirt and to make a light lunch. Salad again, but it was too hot to want to cook—she didn't feel very much like eating either.

She went and knocked on Holden's study door when the meal was ready, and went in to see he was seated at a huge desk with some papers in front of him. He glanced up—she found she didn't like the idea of him working every day.

'Do you have to work every day?' The words had left her before she could stop them, and she was horrified to hear that she sounded quite concerned.

She thought he might laugh at her, but he didn't. Instead, he gave her expression some serious thought. 'If it upsets you, I won't,' he replied evenly after a moment.

Upset her? Rubbish! 'I'll get over it!' she said dryly, then added, 'Your salad's going limp,' and left him to follow or not, as he pleased.

Somehow she felt inwardly scratchy over lunch. Jazzlyn knew this was most unlike her, and, rather than inflict her company on him, when Holden suggested they might take a swim once their lunch had gone down, she declined.

Up in her room a couple of hours later, she began to ponder about this holiday that had seen her unwind from being strung up to relaxed—this holiday that had seen her and Holden becoming friends. A friendship she had enjoyed—and yet a friendship that had seen her contrarily deliberately deny herself his company, be it dining out or going for a swim.

Leaving her room, she went downstairs, deciding to get some potatoes prepared herself. She had barely got there, however, when in the distance from a side window in the kitchen she saw Holden coming towards the house. She guessed he'd been for that swim. He'd always been going to swim, she realised, whether she joined him or not. So, so much for her cutting off her nose to spite her face!

Good heavens, what on earth had made her think in those terms? The phone rang. She glanced from Holden to the phone—and calculated that it could be several minutes before Holden reached the house. Whereas she might miss speaking to her father or Grace if she didn't answer it.

She picked it up and said, 'Hello,' and then discovered that it was neither her father nor Grace, but that somebody wanted a date with her even if Holden never would.

'I'm free tomorrow evening,' David Musgrove announced. 'I wondered if you were.'

Oh, heck—she'd already put him off once. She felt a touch pushed into a corner. Knowing that David was on duty this weekend, Jazzlyn had somehow never considered that he might ring and she had no excuse ready. 'Actually, I'm not,' she answered.

'You're going somewhere?' David asked, apparently not easily put off a second time. Jazzlyn, loath to lie, was still searching for some way of telling David that she wasn't ready to go out with him again when she glanced at the window. Holden, she observed, was getting nearer the whole time. Then she heard David make five of the two and two he'd put together from her long silence. 'You already have a date?' he enquired.

'Well...' she began, but before she could add 'no' David had done another quick sum.

'Not...Holden Hathaway?' he queried. That niggled her a touch. It was just as if he thought never would Holden stoop to ask her out.

'He has asked me out, actually,' she answered.

'You've been out with him before?'

What sort of question was that? Though she supposed that dinner in London *did* constitute going out with Holden. 'Well, yes,' she admitted, and was left blinking in astonishment when David did some more swift, but totally erroneous figurework.

'You're his steady girlfriend?' he more stated than questioned. Even though she opened her mouth to deny it—the words just wouldn't come. 'Do I thank you or Holden Hathaway that you came out with me last Tuesday?' he questioned, sounding a shade peeved.

'There isn't—er—wasn't anything serious between us then,' she was amazed to hear herself answer!

'But there is now?'

He waited. She would have thought he would have called it a day and hung up long before this. But abruptly she was reminded of Tony Johnstone's tenacity—and the memory of his persistent phone calls was returning to haunt her. And all at once she started to panic.

'Yes,' she confirmed in the panic of the moment. And mixed in with her panic was a confused recollection that Holden had asked her to let him deal with it. Compounding her lie, she actually heard herself telling David, 'Holden and I—we're going steady.'

'That rules me out!' David accepted her astonishing statement, having assessed the situation even as a retraction started to hover on her tongue. 'Be happy, Jazzlyn,' he bade her, and, before she could voice her retraction, he was gone.

Some small sense of the enormity of what she had done began to hit her as she saw Holden come round to a side door. Without thinking, acting solely on instinct, knowing only that she was not ready to see him, couldn't face him, she rocketed from the kitchen, along the hall and up the stairs.

She had nearly reached her room when she heard him come in—thank goodness he couldn't see her. She rather thought she heard him go to take a look in the kitchen, but, expecting that his next move if he'd been swimming would be to come up the stairs to take a shower, Jazzlyn wasn't waiting to hear anything more.

In a flash she was inside her room with her door closed, a different kind of panic taking her as the full horror of what she had just done started to break.

Oh, my stars—this was Holden's home village! His backyard, so to speak. He'd made it perfectly plain he didn't want, nor have any interest in, a steady girlfriend. And what had she just done—made a point of telling someone who probably knew some of the same people as Holden that she was going steady with him!

Perhaps David wouldn't tell anybody. Why would he tell anybody? Because Holden was a person of note, that was why. His friends would be interested in that sort of thing, that sort of news. Eligible bachelor, tied down! Most eligible bachelor—her imagination took off.

She'd have to ring David back. A different wave of panic took over—she couldn't! Oh, the shame of it! He might ask her out again. She didn't want to go. He was a doctor, perhaps he wouldn't tell anybody. Doctor-patient confidentiality! Only she wasn't his patient. Oh, what a mess!

She began pacing up and down, but after a while began to feel hemmed in by her room. She hesitated—and in a moment of courage went back down to the kitchen. Thankfully she had the kitchen all to herself, but she was feeling too stewed up to think of scraping or scrubbing potatoes—they could have pasta. She went and stared out of the kitchen window.

Jazzlyn was still a mass of internal disquiet, oblivious to all and anything else but the growing certainty that she was going to have to ring David Musgrove and tell him of her outrageous lie, when a step in the kitchen behind her caused her to spin round. Holden's glance went straight to her face. 'What's the matter?' he questioned quickly—she had forgotten how sharp he was. She couldn't answer—and he came swiftly over to her, his eyes scrutinising her face.

'Wrong?' she asked huskily, aware she was playing for time.

'Come and sit down,' he instructed. 'You look pretty desperate about something.'

'It—shows?' she whispered.

'You're ashen!' Without more ado he pulled out a chair from the kitchen table, but when he went to take a hold of her arm she moved out of his reach.

She didn't want to sit down, she didn't want his sympathy, because suddenly, blindingly clearly, she realised that not only was she going to have to contact David but she was also going to have to confess the truth of what she had done to Holden!

She didn't want to confess. No way did she want to tell him what she had done. But she knew full well that she was honour-bound to let him know that even now there was a possibility that David was sharing what she had told him with someone.

'I've done something dreadful!' she blurted out in panic after that thought.

Holden eyed her steadily. 'Nothing can be as bad as that,' he remarked calmly, holding her eyes with his. Oh, yes it could. 'Come and sit down and tell me about it.'

She shook her head. 'You're going to hate me.'

'I doubt it,' he smiled. And, as astute as she believed, he persisted. 'So it concerns me?'

She loved his smile. 'Oh, Holden,' she said miserably, 'I don't know how to begin to tell you what I've done!'

'Since I can't see anyone dead or dying lying around, it can't be so dreadful as to cause you all this pain,' he coaxed, and seemed at his most understanding.

But Jazzlyn knew that she couldn't bank on him being so understanding once he knew of his involvement in her lie. 'Naturally I'll telephone David and put everything right!' she rushed to tell him quickly, forgetting completely that Holden didn't have a clue what she was talking about—though not liking at all the fact that some of his understanding seemed to be already going out of his expression at the mention of David's name.

'Musgrove?' Holden questioned a degree sternly. 'What's he got to do with it?'

'Perhaps *you'd* better sit down,' she suggested, feeling suddenly nervous and impatient with herself at one and the same time when it became clear that Holden had no intention of taking a seat. 'You know that t-time you asked me to go to that dinner-dance with you?' she plunged. 'That time in London?'

'I remember it,' he answered, his eyes never leaving her face; if he was foxed about where in thunder this reminiscence was taking him, he gave no sign.

'Well, you know you only asked me to go with you because you were—er—hoping to avoid the attentions of some avaricious female without offending her, well—' She broke off and swallowed, the words refusing to leave her throat.

'Well?' Holden questioned, and she felt not at all any better that he was back to looking a mite more understanding.

'Well, David Musgrove rang, not too long ago, and asked if I was free tomorrow evening.'

Oh, crumbs. Holden's understanding look hadn't lasted long! 'You said you were?' he rapped.

That annoyed her. Who the devil did he think he was? About to tell him that it was none of his business, Jazzlyn swiftly recalled that the matter under discussion was very much his business. She swallowed hard again. 'I told him I wasn't free because…' Oh, heavens! She went hot all over.

'Because?'

Holden was being very patient, she realised. And he had lost that momentary aggressive look—though she had an idea it would return—at full power—when she told him what she had added after she had told David that she wasn't free.

'Because, well, I hardly know how it happened, b-but there was I, not ready to go out with him again just yet, and there was David pushing to know why I wasn't free. Then all of a sudden you were somehow in the discussion—had I been out with you, or something.

It all started to get a bit confused then, because the next I know...' Honest though she was, Jazzlyn just couldn't face Holden as she drew a long breath to tell him the next bit. She turned about and went to stand by the draining board, staring unseeing out of the kitchen window. 'And—and the n-next I know,' she stammered on, 'I'm thinking of Tony Johnstone and the way he seemed to hound me when I wouldn't go out with him—and I started to feel that David might do the same. I panicked,' she confessed. 'Anyhow...' Oh, grief, if there was only some other way to tell this! 'I told him...' She paused, took a deep and steadying breath, and added in a rush, 'I told him that there was something s-serious going on between you and me, and that...' her voice started to fade '...and that we were going steady.'

There, it was out—and she wanted to die. The enormity of having told David what she had—a man who actually lived in the same community as Holden—was threatening to sink her. But, having revealed what she had—her guilt—to Holden, this sophisticated man of the world—this man who could have just about any female—she was ready to go under from the shame of it.

She stood rigid, her hands clenched at her sides as she waited for Holden to pour his wrath down on her. But—it didn't come!

She tensed when she heard him move. And very nearly jumped out of her skin when he came to stand directly behind her and placed his hands on her shoulders.

Jazzlyn didn't want to face him, didn't want to look at him. But in that, it seemed, she didn't have any choice. For, his grip firming, he turned her about. She refused to look up, and found one of his shirt buttons of the utmost interest.

And almost collapsed against him when he spoke, his voice the most gentle she had ever heard it. 'What are friends for, dear Jazzlyn?' he asked softly.

Her head shot up. He didn't look angry. 'You're not furious' she asked huskily.

He shook his head. 'No,' he confirmed.

'You don't hate me?'

'I...' He paused, and looked long and hard into her wide, shining unhappy eyes. 'Who could hate you?'

'Oh, Holden!' she cried shakily, and added bravely, knowing a heap of shame would be her lot, 'I'll ring David, of course, and tell him the—'

'Don't you dare!' Holden commanded abruptly.

'But…' She owned to being a touch bewildered. 'If I don't ring him, he may well tell people you know that, well, what I told him!'

'And if you do ring him, and explain you had a moment of confusion, he's going to ask you out again.'

'He may not!' she argued.

'He will,' Holden said, as if he knew it for a fact. 'And you'll run the risk of getting in a panic again.'

'You make me sound pathetic!'

'After what you've been through! You're not pathetic at all,' Holden declared. She was growing to like him better and better all the time. 'Tell me, honestly,' he pressed, 'do you want to go out with him?'

'No,' she answered, not needing to think about it. 'David Musgrove is a nice enough man, but—no,' she repeated. Somehow she just didn't feel like dating anybody just then.

'Then I forbid you to ring him!'

Her eyes went huge. 'You *forbid*?' she exclaimed. He grinned, and all at once she liked him so well he could forbid her as much as he liked. 'You don't mind that if I don't ring him and put him straight he—and probably a few people you're acquainted with—will think that I'm your steady girlfriend?'

'I don't mind a bit,' he answered easily. 'Not if you don't mind me telling my female—er—followers—that I'm already spoken for.'

Suddenly the air was lighter, after such a wretched fifteen or so minutes. Jazzlyn felt so much heartily better, she just couldn't hold back from telling him, 'Do you know something, Mr Hathaway?'

'I'm always willing to learn, Miss Palmer.'

She grinned, she just had to, just as she had to tell him, 'I think I like you more than any man I know.'

Holden stared at her for a long serious second or two, then the corners of his mouth picked up. 'You're just saying that, he accused, but his head came nearer, and while her heartbeat started to quicken he lightly touched his mouth to hers. To feel his lips against hers seemed to set off a tingling kind of trembling all the way through her. But even while she was experiencing the oddest sensation that her legs were going to buckle at any moment he was turning from her and asking, almost in the same breath, 'What are we having for dinner tonight? Have you decided?'

She was glad to see Mrs Williams the next day. Jazzlyn had been pottering about, studying various forms of life she saw in some rock pools, when she'd decided to return to the house. She knew by then that Mrs Williams had a very nice apartment over one of the converted stables, but Jazzlyn felt that was no reason not to welcome her back with a cup of tea or coffee.

She just made it back to the house as Holden's car pulled round to the rear. 'Have you had a nice break?' she greeted the housekeeper, while Holden extracted Mrs Williams' weekend bag from his car.

'I always have a good time when I go to my sister's,' Mrs Williams replied. 'I was sorry, though, to hear that your father and Mrs Craddock had to shorten their holiday.' She went on to say how dreadfully she was going to miss Rembrandt as she and Jazzlyn went indoors.

Jazzlyn had hoped Mrs Williams' return would bring with it more of a sense of normality. Because she freely admitted that something—she couldn't put her finger on what—was making her feel not quite herself.

It was most odd. While she acknowledged that she felt perfectly fit, and was able to put her loss of appetite down to the abnormally long hot and sunny spell they were experiencing—the heat also causing her not to sleep very well—that feeling of restlessness she had known before was attacking her again.

What was oddest, however, was that that restlessness never seemed to attack when she was in Holden's company. Which made it more peculiar than ever that when he had suggested that they do something together, as he had last night—a stroll after dinner, to walk off the pasta—she had declined.

No sooner had he gone, though, than she had been restless again and wishing she had accepted the invitation. Now was that contrary or not? And yet, prior to this holiday, she would have said she hadn't a contrary bone in her body.

Perhaps it was just that she wasn't very good at holidays? Yet now—contrary again—from being all strung up and tense, she could never remember ever feeling so relaxed and at one with the world.

That new perversity in her nature which she had so recently become acquainted with was dominant again that evening however, when, after Mrs Williams had served a wonderful dinner, Holden asked, 'Am I walking by myself tonight, Miss Palmer?'

He was so cool about it that Jazzlyn knew he did not care one way or the other if she joined him. Not that she *wanted* him to care one way or the other, for goodness' sake. What an absurd thought! Still, all the same, a girl had her pride! 'There's something on TV I've been looking forward to,' she heard herself reply—and added the invention of mistruths to her other recent acquisitions.

She was up in her room an hour later when she heard Holden pass her door on his way out. She wanted to go with him. With no idea what was on TV, she turned the bedroom set on—

and contemplated taking a shower. Perhaps not just yet. She'd leave it until later to get out of the cotton dress she'd put on to wear at dinner. She'd shower at ten, she decided, and went to sit propped up on pillows on her bed—and then became hooked on a documentary.

That was, she *was* hooked, until the picture started to act up. She got off the bed and went to study the various unfamiliar buttons on the set. They meant nothing to her. She tried adjusting the controls on the remote control, but succeeded only in turning off the sound and in making the picture worse. She was not, she freely admitted, much of a television engineer.

Jazzlyn was regretfully just about to accept defeat and give up on the documentary when she heard sounds of footsteps coming along the landing. Holden couldn't have gone for a walk after all! She glanced at the flickering TV. Her father always fixed theirs in seconds—perhaps it was a men's thing.

She was at her door and quickly pulled it open just as Holden was passing. Why she should suddenly feel startled she had no idea. He, of course, observed her startled state.

'As bad as that, was it?'

'What?'

'This programme you were eager to see on television,' he replied, his mouth already starting to pick up at the corners.

TV. Her brain woke up. 'There's something wrong with the set,' she informed him. 'Can you...?'

'I'm marginally better with things technical than I am in the kitchen,' he offered modestly, and as she retreated into her room he followed her in.

Jazzlyn, her expertise in such matters nil, left him to it. She went over to the bed and stood watching from there. Then she found that she wasn't watching what he was doing to the television set but that she was watching him. Her heart seemed to skip a beat just from looking at him. How dear he was. How... *dear*?

As if sensing that she was staring at him, Holden suddenly looked over to her. 'Something the matter?' he asked abruptly, leaving what he was doing and coming over to her.

'Matter?' she queried witlessly.

'You look all—peculiar,' he commented, placing a hand on her arm and looking down into her face.

Swiftly, because she had to, Jazzlyn forced herself to recover. 'You don't look so hot yourself,' she flipped back.

He looked a shade taken aback, but his lips twitched just the same. 'Nothing wrong with your mouth, anyhow,' he drawled, but his glance moved down to her mouth and suddenly his banter, his humour fell away. His other hand came to her other arm, and his eyes were on hers again and he was looking nowhere but deeply into her wide violet eyes. 'It's your vertical hold,' he advised in a throaty kind of voice.

She swallowed, a great emotion welling up inside her. 'I never touched you,' she managed huskily, her face turned up towards him. She wanted him to kiss her.

'The TV set,' he explained softly, and his head seemed to be coming nearer, blotting out the light.

'Oh,' she whispered, and she felt a shudder of wonder, of joy, take the whole of her when, gently, Holden placed his mouth over hers.

Though this time—unlike that hint of a kiss he had traced across her lips yesterday—he seemed to like the taste of her mouth.

She wanted to whisper 'Oh' again, as, gentle still, his hold on her steady but ready to let her go if she so desired, Holden's gentle kiss lingered. And no way did she desire him to stop.

Her hands went to his waist; she didn't seem able to hold back. He broke his kiss. 'I—shouldn't have done that,' he muttered, half to himself.

She didn't want any apology. He still held her arms, seemed, like her, unable to let go. 'Yes, you should.' That open and honest part of her refused to let him feel guilty.

His breath seemed to catch. 'You wouldn't object if I did it again?' he asked. His humour was back—there was so much she admired about him.

'I might object if you didn't,' some part of her, some newly awakened part of her encouraged.

'Hussy!' he becalled her tenderly, and Jazzlyn experienced more heart-thumping joy when, his arms coming about her, he drew her close up against him and once more his head came down.

For ageless moments they stood wrapped in each other's arms, and Jazzlyn was lost to everything but the wonder of it. His gentle kisses were subtly changing, becoming warmer, more tenderly seeking, searching, giving.

She clutched hard on to him, took a totally involuntary step yet closer. 'Have you any idea what you do to a man?' he questioned on a groan of longing, and suddenly Jazzlyn was going dizzy with the fire of emotions that raged through her when his hands began to caress from her back to the front of her.

She felt the warmth of his touch on her ribcage and felt suspended, her breath caught, when, his hold high, she felt the heel of his hand against the side swell of her breasts. She wanted him to touch her, to caress her, and pressed against him, vaguely amazed that she felt no shame.

'Sweet Jazzlyn,' he breathed, then kissed her, and as his gentle hands captured her breasts she had her wish.

How, a short while later, they both came to be lying on her bed, she had no idea. Nor did she have shame either. She loved the feel of his length against her length, this touching of his warmth against her warmth. She closed her eyes from the pure pleasuring of it. She felt his kisses to her throat, felt his hands caressing her back, her breasts through the thinness of her clothing. Felt his caressing of her move down to her behind, felt him pull her closer against him—and went willingly.

She heard a moan of wanting leave him as the lower parts of their bodies seemed to fuse together. She had never known such rapture. Yet she had a moment's hesitation when, unaware of how much her dress had ridden up, she felt one of Holden's hands move high under the material to caress her naked thigh.

That hesitation was brief, though, and was born out of this totally new territory in which she found herself. But before she could strain against him again, and brief though her hesitation had been, Holden—his senses as heightened as hers, she realised—had noticed it.

Her thigh felt cold when he removed his hand. And she felt cold all over when Holden, against his instinctive judgement, it seemed, dragged himself away from her and, with his back towards her, moved to sit on the edge of the bed.

'I've got to go!' he said hoarsely.

She didn't believe it! He couldn't go! Didn't he know what he had done to her? 'You've left your bath water running?' The husky emotion in her voice gave the lie to any notion that she was finding humour in this situation.

'I'm—not thinking straight,' he owned, his voice all gravelly. 'You'd hate me in the morning.'

I wouldn't! I wouldn't, she wanted to protest—but she had been better brought up than that. 'That was some vertical hold,' she managed with what brain power he'd left her with—the horizontal hold unforgettable. 'But—I get the picture.'

He turned to look at her and, placing a gentle hand to the side of her face, smiled. 'I doubt you do,' he said, and leaned over to drop a light kiss on the tip of her nose. He pulled back. 'Are you all right?' he asked—and she knew he was about to leave.

'Given that my education has gone up a notch or five—fine,' she replied, and from somewhere found an answering smile.

He went swiftly, and so did her smile. He, she was fast realising, was a rather fantastic person. Was it any wonder that she had fallen in love with him?

CHAPTER SIX

THE wonder of this new-found love for Holden kept Jazzlyn sleepless for half of the night. This, then, was what had been the matter with her—the reason for her feelings of restlessness when she was apart from him; she had been falling in love with him all the time and hadn't, until now, known it.

But it was there, solid in her head, her heart. It was in every part of her and was, she knew, as if written in stone, there to stay. This love she had for him was unshakable and would never leave her. It wasn't just physical—it went deeper than that. Like some earth-shattering blow it had come to her entirely un-expectedly last night. A minute or so before Holden had kissed her—she had known that she was heart and soul in love with him.

This explained the jumble of emotions within her—that unfathomable something that had been going on inside. The feelings she'd put down to unwinding on this holiday, her feelings of being happy—and out of sorts on occasion too. This explained, too, why, when she quite enjoyed male company, she was averse to dating anyone just then.

This explained why, at the start of her holiday, when she had discovered that Holden was the owner of Sandbanks, she had felt urged to leave. It hadn't been, as she'd believed, solely because she'd felt awkward at being what she considered an uninvited guest, but because some subconscious part of her must have read the warning signs. Those signs which had warned her to go, to put herself out of his orbit, had warned that she was in danger of falling in love with Holden. She had ignored those warnings and had stayed—but now, now she realised it was time to go.

Jazzlyn got out of bed and headed for the shower with one thing above all others crystal-clear in her head—Holden must never know of her love for him. They were pals, friends, and would never be anything more. True, they had kissed each other last night in more than friendly fashion, but... A dreadful thought suddenly struck her. Had she invited that first kiss last night? She had wanted him to kiss her, she knew that—but had it been in her eyes.

Oh, no! Holden knew all about women—and then some. Had he read her look? Worse, had he read her love for him? Jazzlyn went hot all over at the thought—it reinforced the fact that she would have to leave that day.

She felt marginally better when she recalled Holden's question, 'Have you any idea what you do to a man?' He'd desired her, she wasn't so naïve that she hadn't recognised that—so perhaps…dare she hope Holden would think it was just a physical thing with her? Some spark of chemistry which, all circumstances being apposite, they had mutually allowed to ignite.

Oh, she did so hope so! Meantime, though, what was she going to do about her by now habitual early-morning walk? She was dressed in jeans and a shirt, and if she was going she should go now. But, she owned, this morning she did not want to. She knew it was because while desperately wanting to see Holden again she was afraid to.

It took a lot of courage, but only when she realised that if Holden was taking his usual early-morning walk—and why wouldn't he?—

he might pause for a moment to consider why she was not, did Jazzlyn swiftly leave her room.

There was no sign of Holden, however, when she went down the stairs. Half-glad, half-sorry, she left the house. But she hadn't gone far along the shore's edge when she spotted Holden in the distance, coming towards her.

Her insides somersaulted, while a desperate kind of shyness which she had never suffered from before threatened to sink her. Feeling torn between a need to see him and an almost overwhelming instinct to turn about and go running back to the sanctuary of the house, Jazzlyn only just managed to summon up sufficient pride to keep going in a forward direction.

By the time they were within speaking distance she was finding the sea of immense interest. And by the time they were within yards of each other, and regardless that her insides were having a merry old time within her, she was outwardly composed—aloof even.

'Good morning,' she offered formally.

He halted as they drew level, and Jazzlyn—knowing she should walk on by—halted too.

'And a very pretty pink you are this morning,' he observed teasingly.

Oh, she loved him so! 'I don't tan easily,' she countered in her best off-hand manner, knowing he was referring to her sudden predisposition to blushing but terrified of otherwise giving herself away and doing her very best to stay aloof.

She was made aware that her aloofness was noted when, looking down at her, Holden casually drawled, 'You'll be pleased to know that business calls me away for a few days.'

'You're going back to London today?' she asked, somehow managing to hide a feeling of near devastation that in a little while the man she loved would be gone from her life!

'"Needs must when the devil drives"',' he quoted.

Jazzlyn made greater efforts to get herself together. 'That makes two of us on the move,' she put in loftily.

Oddly, though, either he didn't care for her tone or for her decamping when there were still a good few days of her holiday left. For he looked at her sharply, and his tone was short when he challenged, 'You intend to return home today?'

'Late today,' she replied, suddenly starting to get worried that he might suggest giving her a lift. Though, if his short tone was anything to go by, that seemed unlikely. What a confused mess being in love had made of her, though. She had determined to go—yet at the same time wasn't ready yet to leave. 'Perhaps I'll see you around some time,' she trotted out, pain already starting to spear her—and she had not parted from him yet! 'Thank you for your hospitality,' she began formally—but was stopped right there. Holden's shortness with her was gone, and a gentle, reproachful note was in his voice somewhere when he interrupted her speech.

'I thought we were friends?' he lamented ruefully.

Already her backbone was melting. 'What's that got to do with the price of lettuce?' She borrowed the short tone he had abandoned.

'You were supposed to be staying for the rest of this week. Today's Tuesday,' he reminded her.

'So?' She went to move away—no argument.

'This has something to do with last night, hasn't it?' he accused, before she could take another step.

Did he *have* to? 'Last night?' she queried, and aloof didn't describe it as she tried to make out that she hadn't a clue what he was talking about. She steeled herself to look up at him.

His look was gentle, and her heart did a by now familiar flip. 'You're more honest than that, Jazzlyn,' he said softly, and, stretching out, he took hold of her hands in his and asked, his eyes steady on her, 'Do I have to apologise that for a while last night my—masculine urges—got the better of me?'

His touch alone was weakening, and just looking at him Jazzlyn felt weak at the knees. She could only love him more that he was ready to take all the blame for what had sprung into life between them last night, when in actual fact half the blame just had to be hers. But where at one time she would openly, honestly have told him that she was half to blame, this new-found love she had for him made her wary to own up to anything that might give him so much as a hint that she cared for him.

'No, you don't,' she replied, her aloofness thawing a little as, if blame there was, she went the nearest she dared to accepting her portion.

There was a smile in Holden's eyes, she saw, a gentle smile that didn't quite reach his mouth as he confessed, 'I've no excuse—other than I find I'm very attracted to you.'

A pounding began in her heart and started to thunder in her ears. 'You—are?' she managed cautiously.

She was heartily glad she had limited her response when, to show just how much he was attracted to her, he stated quite decisively, 'But I don't want an affair with you.'

'Good!' she retorted smartly—a girl had her pride. 'You're not getting one!'

He laughed, threw back his head and laughed at her emphatic reply—and what could she do? She loved the wretched hound; she joined straight in. 'I don't know when I've ever met anyone as natural as you,' Holden commented, smiling still as their laughter faded.

'Go on—you're only saying that!'

His smile became a grin. 'Do me a favour, Jazzlyn?' he asked.

She sobered. In her heart she knew she would do anything for him. He wanted natural? 'Anything!' she answered, her tone casual, as if knowing he would ask nothing terribly arduous of her.

'Finish off your holiday down here,' he requested.

'Oh!' She hadn't been expecting that. 'W-why?' she asked, knowing in her heart of hearts that she would like nothing better. Weakening thoughts sprang to mind. Holden was going to be away for a few days, so surely she could use those few days to gather up her strength to keep a better guard on her emotions. If she went today, Lord knew when—if ever—she would see him again. Whereas if she stayed and he returned, say Friday, she would see him again—perhaps share a meal with him Friday night, before she left on Saturday.

Without knowing it she had dropped her head to stare unseeing to where her sandalled feet were making patterns in the damp sand. She stopped, stilled, when Holden placed a couple of fingers under her chin and tilted her head up so he could look into her face. 'Because being here has thoroughly relaxed you. Look at you,' he went on softly. 'You were beautiful before, but now—your beauty has an added glow.'

His words, that he thought her beautiful, made her feel even more wobbly at the knees. How she found her voice she didn't know. But her good intentions of leaving later that day were nowhere in her head when, as casually as she could, she answered, 'Well, if you put it like that, what girl could refuse?'

'Splendid,' he said, and studied her face, looked deeply into her lovely eyes, then took her in his arms. Jazzlyn allowed it, because it did not occur to her not to. His head came down and gently he kissed her. Then all too soon he was breaking that wonderful kiss and his eyes were on her face again. 'Be here when I get back,' he said, and took a step away. The next Jazzlyn knew, he had turned abruptly from her and she was left staring after him when he went striding in the direction of the house.

She watched him for many long seconds, but it was only when it dawned on her that he might, just might, turn around and catch her watching him that she turned swiftly about and, as if purposefully, set about going for a brisk walk.

Jazzlyn supposed, in a way, it was a relief that Holden had urged her to stay. She knew she was being feeble, but she had never been in love before. And while at one time she would have made a decision she would have stuck to—there would have been no question that a decision made would be carried through—this love, this love she felt for Holden seemed to make a complete and utter nonsense of the woman she'd thought she was.

Holden was very much on her mind that day. He had gone by the time she returned to Sandbanks, and a dreadful feeling of desolation took her. She just dared not think what it would be like when she no longer saw him again.

Even the weather seemed to have grown cooler now that he wasn't here, but she nevertheless gathered up her rug and sunshade and took herself off to her favourite sand dune. She spent the afternoon with Holden occupying most of her thoughts.

A smile curved her mouth as she recalled his reason for wanting her to stay—because her stay so far had thoroughly relaxed her. 'You were beautiful before,' he'd said, 'but now—your beauty has an added glow.'

In reality, though, and bearing in mind his kindness to her, was it more that—knowing her father wasn't home—Holden wanted her to stay rather than return to a house where she would be alone if Tony Johnstone was still pursuing her?

What a super friend Holden was, she mused, recalling how he had made her promise to let him handle matters if Tony Johnstone tried to make contact in any way. But she knew full well then that it would not be necessary to contact Holden over Tony; she reckoned she could quite well handle Tony herself now.

Before, out of consideration for Tony's feelings, she had been too soft on him. But now she knew what truly being in love felt like, and she was totally convinced that by no stretch of the imagination was Tony in love with her. True love didn't stalk—it respected. That being so, should Tony still be dialling her number when she got home, she was not going to take any more of it, but would tell him precisely what she thought of him and where he could go. She was afraid no longer. If nothing else, loving Holden had done that for her.

Jazzlyn fell to thinking solely of Holden for long stretches of time on end, and he was still in her head when she went to bed that night. She thought she understood now his 'I'm—not thinking straight' last night. His 'You'd hate me in the morning.' He was attracted to her, he'd said so, but perhaps, a logical thinker, he had been trying to think that if there was anything very long-term between his aunt and her father it would be better for them to meet again as friends and not as ex-lovers. He'd most definitely stated that he didn't want an affair with her.

Was it not possible for people to remain friends once an affair was over? She'd have thought that there was a fifty per cent chance of staying friends. Though, since she'd never had an affair, what did she know?

Jazzlyn remembered the way Holden had thrown back his head and laughed at her snappy, 'Good—you're not getting one.' Oh, she loved him so. She fell asleep feeling a shade better than she had for most of the day at the thought of parting from Holden on Saturday. If she was reasoning this correctly he fully expected to bump into her from time to time—at least while his aunt and her father were as close as they were.

Just how close her father and Grace were was made clear to Jazzlyn the next day. Mrs Williams, who was having two prearranged days off, was in town looking for a gift to take to a friend when the phone rang. Nancy, Mrs Williams' part-time assistant, three days a week, was busy elsewhere and would probably expect her to answer it, Jazzlyn realised.

Her heart started to race. To her flustered thinking just then, it would be quite an everyday matter for Holden to ring his housekeeper about something or other. She picked up the phone. 'Hello,' she said in her best casual manner.

'How's my second-best girl?' her father enquired—and sounded on top of the world.

'I've been demoted?' she teased, knowing herself very much loved by him.

'Grace has agreed to marry me!' he answered, and sounded so joyful that Jazzlyn stamped down hard on her instant feelings of unease.

'Congratulations!' she exclaimed sunnily.

'You're—okay about it?' he paused to ask as an afterthought.

To her surprise, Jazzlyn realised that, after that initial feeling of apprehensive misgiving, she was. 'I'm fine about it!' she assured her father earnestly. 'I'm fond of Grace, and the two of you seem—right together.'

'That's what we feel. This past four or five days have shown us that. How Grace put up with Archie Craddock as long as she did defeats me! She deserves much better.' He laughed self-consciously and admitted, 'I know I've made some past mistakes—some of them positive howlers—but what Grace needs more than anything in a marriage is absolute honesty, and whatever my faults, I've always been absolutely honest.'

'I know you have,' Jazzlyn answered. Then her father was putting Grace on the line. 'I'm sure you and my father will be very happy together,' Jazzlyn offered warmly.

'You don't mind?' Grace asked.

'I want you both to be happy,' Jazzlyn replied sincerely.

'We will be,' Grace assured her. 'We've talked and talked about it and both know that we wouldn't get married to each other at all unless we were certain that it would work.'

Jazzlyn spoke to Grace for a few more minutes, then her father was on the line again. Apparently, though they were still at Archie Craddock's house, Grace's former husband was much better and well enough able to look after himself.

'We've decided to leave here on Friday and spend the night at Sandbanks, then the three of us and Remmy can drive back home together on Saturday.'

'You needn't come back specially for me!' Jazzlyn said at once.

'It was never my intention to abandon.you,' her father replied. 'Besides, Grace tells me she always wanted a daughter.' His voice became mock-serious as he told her heavily, 'Kindly allow your parents to know what's best for you.'

My goodness, was he on a high, or wasn't he! Jazzlyn said goodbye to him, realising she had never heard him so happy. She put the phone down and had an instinctive kind of feeling that this time his marriage would work, that he and Grace were right for each other.

Was that, she pondered slowly, what marriage was all about—two people being right for each other? Not that she was ever going to try it, she reflected abruptly. No way! Only...

All of a sudden Jazzlyn was being bombarded by a mass of contradictory thoughts. Perhaps if it *was* the right person. If one could find the right person. Holden was in her head again. She quickly ousted him. Gracious, Holden would never ask her to marry him— nor would she accept if he did, or... All at once Jazzlyn found that her firmly held beliefs about marriage, which had grown up with her over the years, were starting to grow cloudy.

Valiantly she strove to remove the fog from her thinking. For goodness' sake, hadn't she lived through too much of the acrimony that had gone on in her father's relationships and marriages, heard too much of those fractured bitter recriminations, seen too much of the bickering, the attack and counter-attack? Her home had more often than not resembled a war zone!

No, she most definitely didn't want that for herself, and intended to stay well clear of it. Only—dammit—she had never been in love before, and somehow her previous thoughts on the subject were getting turned upside down.

Holden aside, she did not want to tie herself up with any member of the opposite sex—only to have to await the 'fall-out'. Yet her father, who was probably more battle-scarred than most, was contemplating doing that very thing!

Which brought her right back to thoughts of two people being right for each other. And once more Holden was in her head again. Jazzlyn at that point decided that what she needed was a long and vigorous walk—that would soon take the confusion out of her head. Falling in love, she realised, had made her vulnerable to thinking the unthinkable. No, most definitely no. She was never, ever going to marry!

She was on her way out when the phone rang again. Holden? She swallowed, suddenly indecisive about answering it. She had an idea that Holden wouldn't be very well pleased about the news of his aunt and her father. Did he know yet? Was that why he was ringing? Maybe to tell her to pack her bags and leave?

Realising her imagination was having a field-day, but knowing also that if Holden didn't know yet about their respective relatives' news that she was going to have to break it to him, Jazzlyn went to the hall phone. She knew, love him though she did, that should Holden make any sort of disparaging remark about her parent she would soundly defend her father.

Defence of her father, however, was not necessary. After again putting on her best casual manner, she said, 'Hello?' and discovered that the caller was not of the masculine gender.

'Mr Hathaway!' a superior voice demanded, clearly expecting someone to run and fetch him.

Jazzlyn did not like the caller. Her superior tone she could take in her stride, but the searing jealousy that tore into her that some hoity-toity sophisticated-sounding female wanted to speak to the man she loved was a totally new and shattering sensation. Jazzlyn most definitely did not care for either.

'I'm afraid he's not home.' She remembered her politenesses long enough to give the other woman the benefit of her good manners. Instinct—hard-nosed, defeating instinct—was telling her that the woman was close to Holden—she couldn't be his PA; she'd know he was not at home.

'Where is he?' questioned the voice imperiously.

Get her! 'Who's calling?' Jazzlyn asked, riled before she started and not ready to give out information to any self-important female.

Her question was not taken kindly. 'Who are you?' the voice demanded frostily. 'His housekeeper?'

Jazzlyn did not take kindly to the cold, patronising manner. Whoever the female was, nobody had the right to address Mrs Williams in that tone. It annoyed her. 'Actually,' she replied, jealousy and annoyance on the rampage, giving her *carte blanche* to make free with the conversation she'd had with Holden last Sunday, 'I'm Holden's girlfriend.'

A stunned silence followed. 'You're his…?' The woman recovered. 'You live there?' she questioned hostilely, acid in every syllable. 'You're saying you're his *live-in* girlfriend?' Her very air said that she didn't believe it for a minute—and that niggled Jazzlyn some more.

'I'm not here to do the dishes, that's for sure,' she answered—and the line went dead.

It didn't take long for Jazzlyn to be absolutely staggered at the realisation of what she had done! As her anger against the supercilious caller started to fade, so Jazzlyn grew all hot and bothered about what had happened.

Annoyance aside, jealousy, she realised, was one almighty dickens of an emotion! While it went without saying that Holden had women-friends—and she didn't want to think of the closeness of those 'friendships'—Jazzlyn knew only that she did not care at all for any of his women ringing Sandbanks while she was there. But—she swallowed hard—that was no excuse for what she had done.

In panic she tried desperately to remember word for word how her conversation with Holden had gone last Sunday. But in remembering she could find nothing in his light-hearted statement that *he* would tell his female followers that he was already spoken for which would allow *her* to tell any of his 'followers' that he was living with someone! Oh, what in thunder did she do now?

Coping with jealousy was something she'd never had to experience before, and living with it she found was no easy chore. But that was one problem, and it still didn't address the other problem—what on earth did she do to correct the impression she had given Holden's female caller?

Well, hardly 'impression'! 'You're saying you're his *live-in* girlfriend?' the insufferable woman had asked—but Jazzlyn wondered, in all honesty, what sort of 'impression' she had expected her answer of, 'I'm not here to do the dishes, that's for sure' to give. Jazzlyn faced it—she could not have confirmed she was Holden's live-in girlfriend more had she stated outright that she was. She supposed it was a natural assumption—since she was in Holden's house and had answered his phone and said she was his girlfriend—for the 'follower' to assume that she was the 'live-in' variety. But that in no way excused her confirming it.

Oh, heck—should she ring him and tell him what she'd done? She didn't have his office number! Chicken! She could find it—and anyway Mrs Williams would have it. Just the same, Jazzlyn shied away from the notion. But a minute or so later she realised that the frosty-voiced woman might well have Holden's office number—since she had the Sandbanks number, she must have. What if she rang him and told him of their conversation? Oh—perish the thought!

Jazzlyn kept well away from the phone. On the basis of this being a working day, she calculated that Frosty Voice must have tried Holden's office before she'd rung Sandbanks. Therefore, it seemed fairly obvious that Holden must be doing business away from his office that day.

But Jazzlyn was restless. She couldn't settle. She went to the drawing room. From there she went upstairs to her room. She went back down to the kitchen and did some washing. She was on her way back indoors after pegging her laundry out on the clothesline when she heard the phone start to ring.

No! Startled, hunted—she didn't want to answer it. It hadn't been him the previous two times when she'd thought it would be him, so why should she think it would be him now? You know very well why, nudged her guilty conscience. She wished Nancy would answer the phone. She wished Mrs Williams was home.

'Hel-lo,' she said on a gasp of breath as she flattened the coward her actions had made of her and nervously picked up the phone.

'You've been rushing?' suggested a voice that she at one and the same time was desperate to hear and not to hear.

'I was outside when the phone started to ring,' she replied, knowing she was pink, knowing—if indeed Holden's purpose in calling was not to castigate—that she was going to have to confess. But she wasn't ready yet to bring coals of wrath tumbling down on her head. 'Did you want to speak with Mrs Williams?' She who up until then could never remember using such tactics attempted to de-

lay the moment of her shaming retribution.
'I'm afraid she—'

'Can't I take a minute out of my full day to
check if my good friend Jazzlyn is enjoying
the sea, the sand and the sun?' he interrupted
her lightly.

Jazzlyn gulped silently—Frosty Voice
hadn't been in touch with him yet, then? 'Er—
I think—er—' She broke off, her voice gone.
Words were there, but no sound to utter them.
The pause stretched.

'You have a problem?' Holden queried.
Already his tone was changing—he'd go spare
when she told him what she'd done!

'I—um…'

'You—um?' he encouraged.

'I—um—think you might have second
thoughts about—um—my being your good
friend, when I—er—tell you what I've done,'
she managed at last to get out.

Silence—then that teasing note she loved so
was there in his voice. 'Oh, Jazzlyn Palmer.'
He seemed to refuse to believe it could be anything so very terrible—but it was, it was. 'Just
what have you been up to?'

Don't hate me! Please don't hate me! She would have to tell him—she couldn't delay any longer. 'You know that conversation we had last Sunday?'

'Refresh my memory—give me a hint,' he requested.

'The conversation—the one—er—where I was explaining to you why I'd said—um— what I had to David Musgrove?'

'You haven't said you'll go out with him again?' he fired curtly. What had happened to teasing?

'No, of course not. Only…'

'Only?'

'Well, you know you said…' oh, she felt hot! '…you said I should tell your—um—fol- lowers that you're—er—spoken for?'

'I—remember.'

Had he sounded a shade wary? She was committed. No going back now. 'Well—I have!' she said baldly.

'You—have?'

Oh, crumbs. 'There was a phone call,' Jazzlyn explained, and had to get it all said, and quickly—that or slam the phone down. 'The woman asked who I was and…'

'And you said you were my girlfriend?' Holden took up—he didn't *sound* too furious, Jazzlyn felt.

'Are you cross?' she asked.

There was a pause, then, his charm threatening to sink her, he asked, 'Who could be cross with you, little Jazzlyn?'

She felt a by now familiar jelly-like sensation in her knees. 'It—er—didn't...' she coughed '...end there.'

'Oh, my word—you mean, there's more?'

'I don't know who she was,' Jazzlyn prevaricated, and, as jealousy nipped, 'Do you?'

'No doubt I shall find out in time,' he answered slowly.

Jealousy still attacking, Jazzlyn plunged. 'I'm afraid I as good as told her that I'm your *live-in* girlfriend!' she said in a rush. Silence, utter silence. 'You *are* furious?' she suggested faintly.

He ignored the suggestion, and instead asked mildly, more to himself than to her, Jazzlyn felt, 'Now why, I wonder, would you do that?' Tell some female over the phone that she was his live-in girlfriend? Because I was screamingly jealous, that's why! It was her turn to remain silent. Wild horses couldn't drag that sort of admission from her. To her gratitude, Holden wasn't pursuing his question, but was commenting, 'I've never had a live-in girlfriend before—tell me, sweet Jazzlyn, am I enjoying it?'

She wanted to laugh. Relief washed over her. He wasn't furious with her! Nor had he ever had anyone to live with him! 'It's the most tremendous fun!' she laughed.

'On that happy note, I'll leave you and get some work done,' Holden said. 'Goodbye, my dear co-habitee.' He sounded as light-hearted as she suddenly felt.

'Bye…' she replied, and put down her phone. '…my darling,' she added.

Jazzlyn was full of euphoria for the next five minutes as she relived again and again her wonderful conversation with Holden. Another five minutes passed while she drifted along on a tide of sublime well being. She even found she was idiotically smiling—then suddenly it hit her! Oh, heavens—she hadn't said a word to Holden about her father's phone call! How *could* she have forgotten?

The warmth went out of her day and her smile vanished without trace. She should have told Holden—she should, she should! It was blatantly obvious that he didn't know that his aunt was to marry her father. *Never* would he have sounded so pleasant-tempered had he already known.

Oh, heck, having fallen from the euphoric sublime to the stark, unhappy depths, Jazzlyn was never more certain that when Holden *did* know he was most definitely going to be totally against the match!

CHAPTER SEVEN

THE more Jazzlyn thought about it, the more convinced she became that Holden was not going to like the idea of Grace marrying her father. That thought went to bed with her, and it was in her head when she awakened the following morning. She remembered how he had only called at their home in the first place because of the protective feelings he held for his aunt. No, most decidedly he was not going to like it.

Jazzlyn tried to be angry about that, but she loved Holden and, given her father's track record, she couldn't help but see any marriage between their two relatives from Holden's viewpoint.

She wondered if he knew—by now. Yet as she got out of bed she just couldn't regret not having told him when he'd phoned yesterday. That phone call had ended so happily—she wanted to remember it always, his tone of voice, his teasing.

She went and stood over by the window, looking out. It looked like being another beautiful day. She left the window to go and have her shower, but returned to her room in pensive mood. She felt the urge to go for her usual early-morning walk, but perhaps she'd be better employed getting her belongings together.

Jazzlyn got out her suitcase—she'd be leaving the day after tomorrow anyway. And anyhow, despite Holden specifically asking her before he left to stay and finish off her holiday, she had a feeling he wouldn't be feeling so philanthropic once he heard the news.

It was with a heavy heart that Jazzlyn completed most of her packing. She felt close to Holden here in his home. Once she left, Lord knew when she would see him again.

There was every possibility that she would see him at her father's wedding—whenever that might be. From what she'd witnessed, Holden was too fond of his aunt—as well as being too much of a man—to decline to attend on what would be a happy day for Grace. But to see him once every plum harvest was going to be hard to bear.

Feeling on the brink of tears, Jazzlyn swiftly closed her case and placed it down in a space next to the wall, then hurried down the stairs. Mrs Williams was there before her, busy in the kitchen, having already come over from her own apartment.

'I thought this was your day off!' Jazzlyn protested, observing that the kettle was already starting to boil.

'I'll just make your breakfast, then I'll—'

'I'll make yours,' Jazzlyn said firmly, and was glad to have the housekeeper to chat to for the next fifteen minutes. It kept her own thoughts at bay.

Once she had waved Mrs Williams off, however, despairing thoughts returned to attack her again. She might never see Holden again before the wedding! Holden had said that business called him away for a few days, which meant that he wouldn't be back at Sandbanks until tomorrow at the earliest, if then. Tomorrow evening, if at all, Jazzlyn judged—and she just didn't know any longer whether to obey her heart and stay, or whether to take notice of her head, her pride, and go.

But pride was feeble when up against love—and, since it seemed she was looking for excuses to stay, Jazzlyn found a tailor-made one. Nancy wasn't due today, and, since Mrs Williams wouldn't be back until later that evening, she had handed over a couple of house keys so that, should Jazzlyn wish to go out, she could secure the house. So, unless Holden phoned and ordered her out, she had no option but to stay until Mrs Williams returned tonight, when she could hand her keys back to her.

That being so, far later than was usual, Jazzlyn locked the door behind her and took herself off for her morning walk. She'd walked this beach with Holden, she reminisced, and recalled the way—the mad, idiotic way—they'd taken a dip in their clothes. Remembered too the way she'd also seen him suave, sophisticated in a dinner jacket. Oh, how she loved him.

Jazzlyn was still loving him, still remembering him—soaking wet, uncaring, laughing—loving him in every mood when an hour later she was retracing her steps. Her eyes misted over. She didn't want to go; she never wanted to leave. And yet she must.

With her head bent in deep and unhappy thought it was some while before she chanced to look up and into the distance of where she was going. Then her heart started to pound. She was the only person at Sandbanks today! But someone else was there—had just arrived, perhaps.

Jazzlyn swallowed on raw emotion as the figure she'd observed in the distance near the house began to walk clear of the building. He—and she was sure that the tall figure *was* a he—was heading her way, walking towards her.

Oh, somebody help her! Was it Holden? He must have left London extremely early to get here by this time. Had he come personally to tell her 'You know that bit about finishing off your holiday? Forget it!'? Oh, how she wished she'd listened to her head and gone. The indignity of it!

With the male drawing nearer all the time, and Jazzlyn walking towards him, it soon became obvious to her from his way of walking, from the proud way he held his head, that it was indeed Holden.

She tried to think up some smart remark, some pride-salving 'I thought I'd have one last look at the sea before my taxi arrives' type of remark. But by the time they were within talking distance her brain seemed to have seized up.

Holden didn't seem to have very much he wanted to say to her either initially, because as they drew level they both halted, and he stared down at her, and she stared up at him, he said not a word. He was unsmiling. This was it—Jazzlyn braced herself to be slung out on her ear. But—it didn't come.

'Thought, with Mrs Williams away all day, you might care for a little company,' he remarked after long, long moments of not saying anything but just standing there scrutinising her face.

Relief flooded through her at terrific pace. She flicked her glance from him so he shouldn't see how it affected her that, instead of the hostility she'd fully expected, Holden sounded just the same as he had on the phone yesterday—friendly and teasing.

'W-when did you get here?' she asked when she thought she could find any sort of a voice.

'Just now,' he answered. 'How are things with you?'

'Fine,' she replied. 'Fine,' she said again, flicking him a glance.

He smiled then, and she adored him. 'Is my live-in girlfriend going to make me a cup of coffee?' he asked.

'Now?' Perhaps he meant when he'd finished his walk. His answer was to turn in the direction of the house. They began walking towards it. 'Did you find out who she was?' Jazzlyn asked.

'I did,' he answered, as smart as ever and immediately on her wavelength.

'Was she angry?' she asked, loving him quite desperately, feeling jealousy over yesterday's woman caller like a physical pain yet needing, painful though it might prove, to know everything.

'We said goodbye,' Holden answered—and sounded extremely cheerful.

'I'm sorry,' she apologised.

'I'm not,' he replied, and seemed so unconcerned that Jazzlyn started to forget everything save that he was there. If he was staying—and with his offer of his company while Mrs

Williams was away, it seemed likely—then she was going to enjoy her day with him. By the sound of it, he wasn't throwing her out. She needed, wanted, some time with him. Greedy it might be, but if there was a chance she was going to grab at that time with him.

It came to Jazzlyn when they reached the house and made for the kitchen that she was feeling so elated she was going to have to doubly guard every word and every look. She'd just about die if Holden guessed at just so much as a quarter of what she felt for him.

'Coffee!' she said, and, turning her back on him, she busied herself making it just how he liked it.

'Can I help?' he offered.

She laughed. 'Why change the habits of a lifetime?'

'Slept in the lemon grove, did we?'

She laughed again and almost said 'I love you too', but by the skin of her teeth managed to hold back. She was going to have to watch it. The way she was feeling inside, any such joking remark was going to come out sounding utterly sincere. She busied herself with the coffee.

Holden carried the tray into the drawing room when it was ready, and it was only when they were both seated opposite each other, with their coffee cups on a table between them, that Jazzlyn, her emotions well hidden, dared another look at him.

'You look tired!' she exclaimed without thinking.

He was looking at her. 'I'm a very busy man,' he replied solemnly—but there was devilment dancing in his eyes.

'You work too hard!' she reproached him. Grief—she sounded like his granny! 'Or is it play?' she questioned, jealousy slamming concern on the head.

'What sort of thing is that to suggest to an upstanding member of the community?' he lobbed back at her, and, despite her feelings of jealousy, it was so good to see him, to be with him, that she just had to smile. Then—she remembered. Her smile faded.

'Er—have you heard from Grace recently?' Even though she didn't want to ask the question, she just knew it could be evaded no longer.

'We spoke on the phone yesterday,' he replied. Just that and nothing more, but the devilment had gone from his eyes.

'You know, then?'

'About your father's plan to marry her?'

'It's a mutual arrangement!' she bridled in spite of herself.

'Did I say it wasn't?'

'You said—' Jazzlyn broke off. She didn't want to fight with him; she just didn't. 'This is your day off. Shall we row now or later?'

'Who wants to row at all?'

'I could put more sugar in your coffee!' she offered.

'You're asking to have your wrists slapped—although alternatively,' he added after a moment, 'I could punish you with a kiss.'

Please! 'I'll settle for a slapped wrist.' She shrugged off-handedly. But she was totally in earnest when, looking at him, her smile gone, she went on solemnly, 'Seriously, Holden, I think they're right for each other.'

'You know so much about it?'

'I know my father. Yes, he's had a couple of failed marriages, and I'm not apportioning blame because, apart from the acrimony and yelling I witnessed as more or less a daily part of life, he—'

'They've hurt you!' Holden suddenly cut in.

'Who?' she asked, startled.

'Your father—his women. They've—'

'He didn't have a harem!' she erupted.

'What he did have was charge of a growing and sensitive child!' Holden returned angrily. 'Does he have any idea of what he's done to you?'

'He's done nothing...'

'He, his women, the strife in your life at a vulnerable age, have all added together to make you afraid to trust,' Holden cut in again.

'No, they haven't!' she interrupted hotly, and was on her feet—she didn't want any coffee.

'You've changed your mind about never getting married, then?' He was on his feet too, stepping round the table—and she hated him.

She wanted to run away, only she was made of sterner stuff than that. She looked down to her feet. 'No,' she whispered, and had never felt so miserable in her life.

'Aw, come here!' Suddenly Holden's arms were stretching out for her. Jazzlyn, her heart thundering against her ribs, remained rigidly still.

Much good did it do her. He took the small pace needed and she felt his arms come about her, urging her to rest against him. She held out for as long as she could. Did good friends act in this way? She didn't know. She didn't seem to know anything any more. Except…that his arms seemed to be a haven.

Against her will, she went in close and rested her head against his chest. She didn't want to argue with him. And in fact being held by him, being in his arms, was such utter bliss she was fast losing sight of what they had been arguing about. For a short while she knew peace.

Then she felt what she thought was a light kiss to the top of her head. She felt confused—some part of her telling her to move while another part of her was positive she must stay exactly where she was in the haven of his arms. She stirred. It seemed to break some kind of spell.

While still holding her, Holden took a step back. 'Fancy a swim?' he asked.

She blinked. A swim! They'd been in the middle of a fight! She looked up at him. How dear he was to her. 'You're a pig!' she said.

'I know,' he agreed, and his grin was coming out. 'Shall we go and get our trotters wet?'

Was there ever such a man? She just had to laugh. 'Be back with you in five minutes,' she agreed, and left him to go up to her room to change. Holden had intimated that he thought her sensitive, but Jazzlyn reckoned that he was pretty sensitive himself. He'd seen at once that she was upset and, rather than push home his argument, he had taken a hold of her and given her a hug better.

She was going to have to watch it, she re-endorsed. He'd soon picked up the fact she was unhappy. She felt vulnerable suddenly, and was torn between a desire to run to join him for a swim and a reluctance to do anything of the kind.

The thought that after today she would not see him again until Grace and her father's wedding spurred her into donning a swimsuit. Though—perhaps from her feelings of vulnerability—Jazzlyn chose to don her one-piece swimsuit rather than her bikini.

Armed with a large and fluffy towel, Jazzlyn left her room and went downstairs to find Holden there before her. He had changed too, and she brought her eyes swiftly away from the broad expanse of his manly chest. She saw his glance rest on her long length of leg—and felt breathless for no reason.

'Quick-change artist,' she said.

'Great legs!' he countered.

'Can't complain,' she grinned modestly— and he was ushering her out of the door.

By an unspoken mutual consent the marriage of their relatives was not mentioned again. Jazzlyn certainly had no wish to bring it up and so restart hostilities all over. It was heart-wrenching not to be friends with him, and she never wanted not to be friends again.

So they swam, dived and generally enjoyed the water until Holden decreed she'd burn if she stayed with her shoulders exposed to the sun any longer. She didn't want to go back to the house, but wanted to stay where she was, with him.

'You're just interested in your lunch,' she complained.

'Now that you mention it,' he agreed.

They went back to the house and separated on the upper landing when he walked past her door to his own. She could hear the plumbing of his shower before she'd so much as wriggled out of her wet swimsuit. Quick-change artist had she said? She smiled as she stood under her own shower and shampooed the sand from her white-blonde hair and her body.

Her newly washed hair was shining when, having used the hairdryer in the bathroom to good effect, and dressed in lightweight trousers and a tee shirt, she later went kitchenwards.

Once there, seeing Holden already at work wielding a grill pan, she staggered against the doorway and clutched at her heart. 'You're *cooking*!' she gasped.

'How does bacon sandwiches and ice cream sound?' he asked lordily.

'Magnificent!'

'You may lay the table,' he granted.

That lunch was the best meal she had ever tasted. Never had bacon sandwiches been so utterly sublime. Never had a scoop of ice cream been so superbly spooned into her dish. It was true—she loved him.

They spoke of nothing—it was witty, funny, and she laughed a lot. They decided against using the dishwasher, and Jazzlyn washed while Holden dried. And at his closeness she suddenly sensed she was in danger of giving away just how very deeply she cared for him.

'That's everything, I think.' She found her voice, taking a glance around the kitchen. 'I'd better go and rinse my swimsuit out.'

She left him. It was his day off. Agreed, he'd said he'd come to keep her company while Mrs Williams was gone, but Jazzlyn felt sure he must want some time to himself.

Up in her room, she rinsed an already rinsed swimsuit and cleaned her teeth, and wondered what else she might do. What she wanted to do was to go and seek Holden out. But she didn't want to overload him with her company.

She started to ache to see him again, and determinedly tidied her already tidy room. She was feeling vulnerable and scared, as if some sixth sense was warning her to keep out of Holden's way. But why, when she loved him so? Contrary to what she wanted to do, she turned her back on the dictates of her heart, which would have seen her leaving her room, and went to stand looking out of her bedroom window.

A movement to the left of her caught her eye, and a mixture of relief and disappointment assailed her. Holden came further into view— he was taking himself off for the walk which he had cut short when he had met her earlier that day. She wanted to go with him.

Instead, with her head filled with thoughts of Holden, Jazzlyn changed into her bikini, added her shorts, and with a rug over her arm, headed for the sand dunes.

It did not surprise her in the slightest to find when she got there that she had forgotten to bring the over-large umbrella which she used as a sunshade. It was not a problem. She set the rug down in a shaded spot and, making herself comfortable, opened her book.

A half an hour later she gave up all pretence of trying to read. She had turned over perhaps two pages, but could not remember a word of what she'd read; if she had read she would have known the present paragraph off by heart she must have read it so many times.

She ached inside for Holden. Was this how it was going to be? The future seemed bleak without him. And yet she could not wish that she had never met him. He was sensitive, kind and, yes, she knew, he could be sharp too. Yet even when he was being sharp, angry, as he had been a few hours ago in the drawing room, he'd seen she was unhappy and had relented, had taken her in his arms. And for a short while she had known peace.

She wanted to know that peace again. To be held safe again by Holden. She— Her thoughts halted abruptly. She heard a sound nearby— and the next moment Holden appeared.

Aware that her dark glasses were not so dense that Holden could not see her eyes, even as she smiled she was at pains to guard her expression.

'Want to be alone?' he questioned, taller than ever as he stood above her, looking down at her. He was clad in shorts and a shirt, and with long masculine legs within touching distance Jazzlyn suddenly could not bear that he should go.

'Love some company,' she invited, and as Holden came and shared her rug she sat up and discovered the odd bird flying overhead of great interest. 'Aren't the gulls majestic?' she commented, feeling the need all at once to make conversation.

'Regal in their gliding flight,' he observed, and she had the oddest notion that he knew of her sudden shyness and was teasing her.

'Did you enjoy your walk?' She swiftly changed the conversation, and could have groaned out loud, because then she felt she just had to add, 'I saw you set off from my bedroom window.'

'A true friend would have come with me,' Holden remarked casually.

'I *am* a true friend!' she objected.

He glanced her way. 'I suppose you are,' he grinned, and stretched out his long length on the rug.

Oh, she loved him so. Jazzlyn followed suit, and lay down too. She closed her eyes and just had to ask. 'Do you have many women-friends? Er—I don't mean *that* sort—you wouldn't tell me anyway—but—um—women like me...' she wished she'd never got started '...who you're friendly with?'

She'd thought he wasn't going to answer, but before she could begin to be embarrassed that he might consider her prying, he returned lightly, 'Oh, sweet Jazzlyn. I don't think I know anyone quite like you.'

'Do I feel complimented or otherwise?'

'You're sunshine on a rainy day!' he said— and she went all wobbly inside.

'You're only saying that!' she laughed—and picked up her book, needing seriously to be doing something. She put it down again—it suddenly became of vital importance that she didn't waste a moment of this so short a time with him. 'I expect, though, that you know a lot of women?' Her tongue just seemed to run away with her.

'I expect I do,' he drawled, and that jarred her jealousy, though that jealousy was a little negated when, with good humour there in his voice, he added, 'But then, I've been around a while.'

She sat up, feeling oddly fidgety. She looked down at him; he had his eyes closed. 'It doesn't show,' she murmured demurely. He opened his eyes.

'You're asking for trouble,' he commented.

'How old are you?' she asked.

'Thirty-six,' he replied, turning on to his side to look up at her, his expression taking on a serious look as he asked lightly, 'Does thirty-six make me too old to be your friend?'

No way. 'I love thirty-six,' she laughed, and felt hot all over. The kind of friend he wanted kept love out of it. 'Will we still be friends when *I'm* thirty-six, do you think?' she asked in a rush.

'We'll make a pact, here and now, to have dinner together on your thirty-sixth birthday,' he promised.

She laughed. It sounded wonderful. 'Oh, I love daft conversations,' she grinned.

'Woman, you've no soul!' he told her heavily, and as her grin fell away she felt a sudden kind of electric tension in the air. She stared at him, at his mouth, his eyes, and saw his glance flick to her mouth. Then he was flicking his glance away, taking in the fact that the sun was full on her, and as he sat up she realised that if there was any tension in the air she was the only one feeling it. For his voice was the most casual she had ever heard it when, his glance moving to her uncovered shoulders, he stated, 'The sun's moved round. Where's your sun cream? I'll put some on your shoulders.'

The sunshade was not the only thing she had forgotten, she realised. 'I've forgotten to bring it with me,' she answered, and was glad she had forgotten it. She was feeling extremely vulnerable. If Holden so much as laid a finger on her bare skin, she had a feeling she would want to fling herself into his arms. 'I'd better go in,' she added reluctantly.

'No need,' Holden said. He had an answer for everything, apparently, because the next she knew he was unbuttoning his shirt and shrugging out of it. She stared at him, at his naked chest—she wanted to touch him.

'What are you doing?' she asked a mite croakily. But she had her answer when, on his knees, his body blocking out the sun, he draped his shirt around her shoulders. 'W-what about you?' she questioned shakily, feeling the warmth of his shirt, the warmth of him.

'Your skin's fairer than mine.' He smiled down at her. But something was happening to him too. Her senses suddenly never more heightened; she knew it. He went to button his shirt at her throat, but didn't quite make it. For as his hand brushed her skin it seemed to electrify them both. 'Jazzlyn. Oh, Jazzlyn,' he groaned, his hands moving beneath his shirt and taking a firm grip on her shoulders.

She sensed as his hands gripped her that he was striving to keep a sense of proportion, a sense of control. But she didn't want him to keep control. She ached to be in his arms. Just one more kiss. Just one more kiss to remember.

'I…' she gasped.

'What?' He stared down at her, into her warm violet eyes. 'What, Jazzlyn?' he asked, as if sorely in need of help.

'I wish—you'd kiss me,' she answered, and even as she recognised that that was not the kind of help he had been after she felt his grip on her shoulders tighten. Then she heard a groan escape him, and the next moment she was on the receiving end of her wish.

He moved his head, his arms came around her as he reached for her and, as his shirt fell from her shoulders, his mouth met hers. It was a long, lingering kiss. A thoroughly satisfying kiss—and yet, when Holden pulled back to look into her eyes, she wanted more.

'Have you any idea what you're doing to me?' he asked throatily.

If it was anything like what he was doing to her, Jazzlyn reckoned that she had a fair idea. She smiled, and, fair being fair, decided it was her turn to kiss him. She did not hesitate but went forwards. Holden met her halfway, and again she knew the utter bliss of his mouth against hers.

Holden held her firmly to him as again and again they exchanged kisses. She wanted to feel and hold him, and moved her delicate hands over his naked back, her heart threatening to explode within her at the emotion she was feeling.

In turn, Holden, while holding her close against his nakedness, caressed with gentle hands over her shoulders, over her back. He traced kisses down her throat and to her shoulders, and pulled back to kiss down to the swell of her breasts and the hollow in between.

Then his lips were on hers again, mobile, giving, taking. There was no one else in the world then save, in that private part of the sand dunes, their two selves. Her heart raced as Holden's sensitive fingers caressed her back. They came into contact with the fastening of her bikini top, and halted. He kissed her. 'May

I?' he asked, and she knew that he was asking permission to remove her bra.

'It's—er—not a liberty I allow everyone,' she answered, and then, her head away with the fairies, 'But you're special.'

'My little one,' he breathed exultantly, but did not straight away undo the clasp. He kissed her tenderly, his hands caressing to her shoulders and back down again, before he removed her bra.

The overwhelming, fire-igniting feeling that deluged her when Holden pulled her to him and she felt his naked chest against her naked breasts threatened to swamp her.

'Something's happening to me!' she gasped, and felt cold all at once when Holden pulled away from her.

'Is it worrying you?' he asked, his tone quiet, his eyes watchful on her face.

She shook her head. 'I—want it to happen.' She gave him full permission. 'It's just that it's—new. And I...and I'm not sure about—er—things.'

'I'll guide you, sweet love,' Holden breathed, and at these words 'sweet love'

Jazzlyn experienced such a rush of emotion she was eager to go wherever he led.

She kissed him, and knew utter and sublime bliss when he held her close and kissed her, and his caressing hands gently and tenderly moved round to capture her full, throbbing breasts.

'Oh, Holden,' she whispered.

'You're all right?' he questioned, his hands cupping her breasts, his fingertips making a nonsense of her as they teased and played with the throbbing hardened peaks.

'Never better,' she replied. 'May I touch you?'

'My body's yours,' he smiled—and she adored him.

She pulled back and stroked his chest, intimately touching his nipples. She almost told him that she loved him, but held back. Then Holden was pulling back to stare in fascination at her beautiful breasts.

Shyness, an unexpected shyness, all at once overtook her. She pulled in close. 'I'm sorry—I need a second or two to—um—get used to—um...'

'Don't worry, little love,' Holden smiled. 'Come here,' he added, and, holding her close up against him, shielding her body from the sun with his body, he brought her to lie down.

With his body half over hers, it was only when she felt the gentle touch of his kiss to her eyes that she realised her sunglasses had long gone. She stretched up and kissed his eyes.

He smiled, and traced kisses down to her breasts. She clutched on to him as his mouth closed over her breast and she felt his tongue tantalise the wanting tip.

'Oh, Holden,' she gasped, pressing her body against him and hearing his groan of desire. 'Am I wanton?'

He laughed gently. 'You're wonderful,' he said, and she kissed him, and bent and kissed his nipples. 'And a tremendous pupil,' he whispered, then bent his head to kiss down to her waist.

What a wonderful teacher he was! Jazzlyn was lost to everything but the man she loved when she felt him removing her shorts. He moved away, and when he joined her again she knew he had disposed of his shorts too. They both had small clothing between them. He kissed her, kissed her breasts and belly. And then he kissed back up to her throat.

Oh, how dear he was to her, and how, with this fire he had ignited in her starting to take charge, she wanted him. 'You're not frightened, little one?' he asked, his eyes intent on her face.

She shook her head, feeling too full to speak, knowing only that she loved him and that nothing mattered now save that he made her his. As his hands moved down to her waist so her hands moved down to his waist. She felt his hands at the top of her bikini bottoms and started to move her hands likewise—and then found that, as wanton as she believed herself to be, she had come up against a brick wall of shyness when it came to putting her hands inside his undergarment.

'You've gone shy on me!' Holden tenderly understood, and never had she loved him more.

She smiled at him, and kissed him so he should know that, shy she might be, but she still wanted with all she had for him to make her his. 'I'll get over it,' she whispered huskily, and was tenderly kissed.

Then, gradually, their lovemaking seemed to be entering a new and enchanting phase, as Holden kissed and caressed her, and took her gently spinning on an upward spiral of wanting as he moulded and tormented her breasts, touched her lips with his tongue.

'Holden!' She cried his name, arching her body to him. She heard him groan with desire, his desire urgent as he placed his hands over her behind. 'Holden!' she cried again, rapturously, when he moved her, his hands caressing, so that she lay under him.

'Oh, little love,' he whispered, and, caressing her still, his hands stroked down her body. She gave a nervous and involuntary jerk of movement when gradually, unhurriedly, everything about their lovemaking became incredibly more intimate. 'All right, my darling?' He gentled her—and her love for him rose up and, mingling with the nonsense he had made of her senses, made her speechless for a moment.

But she swallowed on her raw emotion. 'Oh, yes,' she gasped. 'Yes, yes. Oh, Holden,' she whispered urgently, still in that same highly emotionally charged state, wanting to let him know that she would make no demur whatever the intimacy. 'I do love you so!'

Shock waves hit her as soon as the words were out. She went rigid! She hadn't said what she thought she'd said! Had she? Holden didn't believe it either, she swiftly realised, and he was traumatised too. For as he stilled, and she stared disbelieving, dumbstruck, into his incredulous expression, she thought he even seemed to have lost some of his colour from the shock of it.

'What—did you say?' he asked, his voice all kind of strangled in his incredulity.

Like she was going to repeat it! Abruptly, shock waves still assaulting her, panic set in. She was wearing nothing but her bikini bottoms. But as that panic hit home—all notions of making love split asunder—Jazzlyn, her only aim being to get out of there, and fast, would not then have stopped to search for clothes had she been completely naked.

She was grateful, however, that Holden had begun to sit up, away from her in his stunned shock. In the next instant she was away. At a sprint, she was out of there. Racing over the dunes, she went charging towards the house. She didn't stop running until, still in panic, she reached her bedroom.

Only when she realised that she had somehow instinctively headed for the shower—as if to wash away her words, and all memory of her lovemaking with Holden—did sufficient of her panic leave to make room for coherent thought.

She hadn't, she hadn't, oh, she hadn't, had she? Oh, heavens, she knew that she had! Well, that was the end of it. Forget friend. Forget meeting on her thirty-sixth birthday. Tears sprang to her eyes. She brushed them angrily away. Oh, what a fool she was!

Holden didn't want her love. He was too sophisticated to be embarrassed by it, but, from the kindness and sensitivity she had witnessed in him, she guessed that once he'd got over his shock he would expect her to leave. He had made it perfectly plain that all he wanted from her was friendship. He had said outright that he didn't want an affair with her. So, okay, the attraction he'd also said he felt for her had just now got wildly out of hand. But by no stretch of the imagination did he want her love.

Realising that once he'd recovered he might well wait in the dunes to watch her leave, Jazzlyn knew an urgency to be away. She'd just about die if, instead of waiting and watching for her to leave, he came back and suggested he'd give her a lift to the nearest railway station. She… Oh…!

All thought abruptly ceased when, even as she was preparing to leave the shower, the shower door opened and, in the same movement that he reached in to turn the water off, Holden caught a firm hold of her upper arm. And the next Jazzlyn knew she was being hauled out.

Holden had the advantage of her. For, while he was bare-chested, he did have the benefit of a pair of shorts. While she—she was stark naked! A squeak of alarm escaped her—out in the dunes in the fever of their lovemaking she hadn't minded a bit being near naked with him. But now, that fever cooled, she was never more embarrassed in her life.

His face was set. He was determined about something; she could see that. But, for all he wasn't making a meal of her breasts and thighs, she knew her nakedness had registered with him. 'A t-towel!' she spluttered as urgently as she was able.

He grabbed one and pushed it at her. 'We need to talk!' he rapped.

Jazzlyn felt only marginally better for being able to hold some sort of covering in front of her. But, after their wonderful, sensitive love-making, she felt stung by his uncaring tone. 'Obviously it won't wait?' she snapped.

'It won't!'

Oh, Lord. As she'd thought, he wasn't embarrassed at her declaration that she loved him—though she hadn't thought he'd be furious either! 'I'll be down as s-soon as I've dried my hair.' She attempted to delay the moment. No *way*, was she going to have any sort of 'talk' with him that all too clearly hinged on her unthinking, utterly mindless avowal of love.

'*Now!*' Holden insisted forcefully.

That made her angry! How *could* he be so furious after the loving and giving way they'd been with each other? 'In case you hadn't noticed,' she flared, 'I'm stark naked.'

'I noticed!' he replied sharply, and she was sure she saw a muscle jerk in his temple a moment before he turned abruptly about. 'Ten minutes!' he ordered over his shoulder, and strode out.

Ten minutes! Like hell! Jazzlyn wasted a full sixty seconds of those ten minutes in just staring after him when he had gone. Then she heard the sound of his shower running and was suddenly galvanised into action.

She made a hasty rub at her wet hair—no time to use the dryer—and wrapped her hair in a towel while she damp-dried her body— which caused seconds' delay when her clothes wouldn't slip on easily. But eventually she was dressed in shirt and trousers—no time for make-up—and she was getting out of there. Once away from Sandbanks she'd either hitch a lift or call a taxi from the village phone box—which, was unimportant. The main thing was to get out of there without Mr-we-need-to-talk-Hathaway knowing anything about it.

She gave her hair another quick rub and dragged a comb through it, and yanked her suitcase on to the bed and opened it. She had the majority of her belongings already packed, thank goodness. She had a damp swimsuit from this morning's swim... Oh, why on earth was she bothering about that, she wondered as panic took another uncontrolled swipe at her.

On that instant, Jazzlyn decided that anything that wasn't in her case could jolly well stay. And the next few seconds after that she had her case fastened and was on her way with it to the door.

As lightly as she could, given that she was hauling a heavy suitcase with her, Jazzlyn hurried down the stairs. She made it to the hall and turned, intending to slip out of the front door—but, her way was barred.

'Not running out on me, Jazzlyn?' Holden asked evenly. Utterly stunned, she just stood and stared, stupefied that he was at the front door before her—his damp hair testifying that he had also showered any sand from his hair and body. He started to move towards her.

'Would I?' she replied, and, with every intention of doing just that, she did the swiftest about-turn on record and, again hampered by her case, which just then she didn't seem to have the wit to let go of, she raced for the rear door.

Holden was there before her. She stopped, defeated, a yard away from him. And nearly died when Holden, to tell her—as if she didn't know—what all this was about, enquired pleasantly, 'Was it something you said?'

'Get lost, Hathaway!' was the best she could manage by way of retaliation.

'Presently,' he answered coolly. 'Meantime…'

Oh, somebody help her—she had never seen him look so determined!

CHAPTER EIGHT

'WE'LL go to the drawing room,' Holden decided.

Oh, will we! Apparently they would, because even while Jazzlyn, her heart thundering away like crazy, was determined not to go a step anywhere with him, Holden was relieving her of her suitcase and setting it down in the hall. Then, his expression clearly telling her that he would carry her to the drawing room if he had to, he was taking hold of her by her upper arm.

'There's no need for that!' she snapped, jerking her arm out of his grasp.

He studied her. With a narrowed, thoughtful gaze he studied her. 'My word, you *are* agitated!' he remarked calmly.

And she wanted to hit him and hit him, because he was the cause and she was hurting and she knew he was going to hurt her some more—and there was just no need for it. Why couldn't he just let her go—pretend that none of this had ever happened?

Because he wasn't a man for pretence—that was why. 'Huh!' How on earth had she managed to make her voice sound so careless? 'You want to talk—we'll talk!' She shrugged, every bit as though she was not in the least bit agitated.

Jazzlyn walked away from the rear door towards the drawing room, knowing before she started that she was going to deny, deny, deny. Holden, as though not trusting her not to make a dive for the front door, was by her side every step of the way.

'Take a seat,' he invited, once they were in the drawing room, the door closed.

He thought it was going to take that long? Forget the suitcase—she'd be legging it down the drive at the very first opportunity. 'Look, there really isn't any need for this,' she attempted, refusing his offer to take her ease.

'You don't think so?' Those grey eyes were on her face, observing, studying, taking in every look, every nuance.

Oh, help, she had never seen him so resolute, so immovable. She looked away from him, and in some desperation she sought, and found, what she hoped was a change from the conversation on which he was so obviously intent. 'We're civilised people, Holden,' she began, as casually as she could manage, given that she was feeling as breathless as if she'd run a mile. 'I'm sure you, like me, will forget that we ever—we ever...' Oh, hang it! She took a long, steadying breath. 'Anyhow, when we meet again at Grace and my father's wedding, I'm sure neither of us w-would—w-will...' Oh, confound it! '...act in any way to spoil their day.' She dared to look at him—oh, grief. He was staring at her as though he just couldn't believe she was babbling on so about something so totally irrelevant to the issue he wanted to discuss with her. 'Anyway,' she rushed on, feeling hot, bothered and very much in need of that seat he had offered a short while ago, 'Grace has been through one marriage where her husband was untrustworthy. So she needs someone who won't cheat on her—she wouldn't b-be able to take that. My father, now, he would never break her trust; he has never ch-cheated on anyone in his life.' She ran out of steam and glanced anxiously at the door. Then she glanced back to Holden.

Unspeaking, he shook his head—that action, even without the alert look in his eyes, telling her that she'd never make it to the door. 'Most interesting,' he remarked of her unnerved verbosity. 'So why don't we—as civilised people,' he inserted, 'sit down and talk about it?'

Jazzlyn opened her mouth to tell him no, but as he began to move towards her so her agitation got the better of her. She backed away and didn't stop until she came up against one of the three sofas in the room. She could go no further, and, short of confirming that she was scared half out of her wits if she played a dodging game round the back of the sofa, she decided it was far more dignified to do as he suggested.

Once she was seated, however, she did not care at all for the way Holden pushed one of the castered padded chairs close up to her and, sitting himself down, leaned forward to begin, 'Back in those sand dunes a short while ago, you—'

'That's not fair!' she erupted, her panic instant. 'W-we were talking of G-Grace and my father!'

'You were; I wasn't,' he contradicted.

'Yes, well...'

'"Yes, well" nothing!' Holden refused to let her wriggle away from the subject he was set on discussing. 'You've stated that you love me and—'

'Oh, come on, Holden!' she interrupted him at the gallop. 'You know darn well that I'd—I'd never been in th-that sort of—um—situation before.'

His look softened. 'Blame me all you want,' he invited.

Drat him! He knew as well as she that their lovemaking had been a mutual spontaneous happening—no blame to be apportioned on either side. 'I wouldn't do that,' she answered—make the most of it, that's about as honest as I'm going to get. 'But, well, you know more than me that—um—people—women—er—men too, I suppose...' Whew, it was hot in here! '...get—um—sort of carried away at—er—times like that.' She broke off, feeling hot and flustered—while he was cool, and seemed to be watching her very closely.

'That's true,' he conceded.

Jazzlyn started to feel a little better. Quite plainly she realised she could bluff this out. She smiled, and began to feel much more relaxed. 'In the—hmm—heat of the moment, one might say th-things one didn't truly mean,' she commented, feeling more relaxed by the moment.

But she felt immediately on edge again when, even though there was an answering hint of a smile on his mouth, Holden replied 'Might one?'

Was he playing with her? Her smile abruptly departed as all feelings of relaxation rocketed away and tension took over once more. Somehow she was gaining the opinion that never, even in his most—er—heightened moments, would Holden tell any woman he loved her unless he truly meant it. So, what did she know?

What she did know was that, sunk she might be, but pride demanded she did not go down without a fight. 'Of course!' she stated firmly, down but not out. 'I thought...' bluff it, bluff

'...I sort of thought—and as you know I haven't very much experience of this—er—kind of thing—that it was—um—an obligatory thing to say.'

She dared a look at him to see how he had taken her remarks—but she could gauge nothing from his expression. Though that hint of a smile was nowhere about; that was for sure.

'You'd denigrate what happened between us?' he asked harshly.

She was bewildered. 'I don't understand,' she confessed—and wanted the floor to open up and swallow her when he explained.

'What happened between us was spontaneous, beautiful—and true,' he stated sternly. 'There was nothing false or phoney about any of it. I won't have you trying to make out that there was!'

Her backbone threatened to liquidise. It had been everything he said. Their lovemaking had happened because neither of them had seemed able to stop themselves once it had begun. But that he, like her, should think their rapture with each other beautiful made her feel all weak at the knees. But—this would never do!

'I...I lost my head.' She tried bluffing it out again.

'We both did,' he agreed.

Oh, Holden, she inwardly wailed, and tried again. 'Is it any wonder—with you making such a nonsense of me—that—that—er—um—pleasuring me so...' Her face burned; she'd gone scarlet, she knew that she had. She made herself continue, 'That I should w-want to say something that might—only in that moment, of course, give you—um—a little pleasure—not that you...you'd b-be that thrilled...' Her voice tailed off, and as she came to an inauspicious end Jazzlyn knew, when he smiled a sceptical smile, that she hadn't fooled him for a minute.

'You're looking extremely hot, if you'll pardon my saying so,' he remarked softly.

'It's the company I keep!' she snapped disagreeably, not thanking him for drawing attention to her searing blush or the fact that she was feeling all boiled and flustered.

'And you almost had me believing you a moment ago,' he went on, completely as though she had not spoken. 'Except that over these past days and weeks I've got to know a great deal about you.'

Jazzlyn didn't think she liked the sound of that. 'All good, I hope,' she offered sarcastically, determined to keep her end up.

'Most of it,' he answered with a gentle smile. 'In fact, apart from one drawback which...' He paused, and to her mind—and she was watching him as closely as he was watching her—he seemed strangely a little unsure himself as he went on, 'Which I hope to satisfactorily resolve, all of it.'

She didn't want him to smile gently; it weakened her. 'You're talking in riddles,' she accused, suddenly realising that if she didn't soon start going on the attack, instead of being on the defensive all the time, she was going to find herself in very deep trouble.

'Not to me,' he answered, but didn't explain, and instead went on. 'One of the many things I've learned and have appreciated about you, Jazzlyn, is your honesty.'

'Do I thank you?'

'I shouldn't! It's that honesty in you that has me knowing that, despite your dishonest attempts to make me believe you said those

words ''I do love you so''...' He paused, as
she coloured up again, and leaned further forward to stroke a hand down the side of her left
cheek, as if to stroke her pinkened colour
away. Jazzlyn pulled sharply back. She had
enough to contend with without his weakening
tender touch to her skin. But, determinedly, he
would not be put off. 'Despite you trying to
make me believe you said those words out of
some obligation because we were making
love,' he resumed, 'I *know* that you're more
honest than that.'

'Huh!' she scoffed—the best she could ac-
complish. He ignored it.

'I just don't believe, knowing you as I have
grown to know you, that you'd say those
words—whatever the heightened circumstances—unless you meant them.'

Desperately did Jazzlyn want to swallow.
But that would be a dead give-away that she
was having forty fits inside. Bluff. Bluff it out.
'You obviously don't know me as well as you
think you do!' She shrugged—it was a pity she
couldn't meet his eyes. She took another deep
and controlling breath and then, as agitated as
he had observed she was, not to mention that

there were about half a dozen other emotions within her all on the rampage, Jazzlyn started to get angry. So, okay, she loved the brute, but did she have to sit here and take it while he doggedly probed and dissected her most sensitive feelings for him? 'What's the big deal anyway, Hathaway?' she questioned shortly, glad to feel angry, even able to take a look at him—she could tell absolutely nothing from his expression! 'Now that we've both—er—cooled down—from—er—our—um—sandy encounter, I would have thought it totally neither here nor there what either of us said w-while in the throes of—er—um...'

Her voice had run out on her again. And, devil take it, as Holden sat there silently watching her her anger went with it. She made to rise to her feet—she was leaving. Only Holden moved too, and gently but firmly pushed her down again.

'Not yet!' he stated softly. 'I'm sorry you're so uptight, but, contrary to your belief that what you said in those sand dunes is neither here nor there, and your notion that I wasn't, or wouldn't be thrilled by what you let slip at that most emotional time for us—the big deal,

my dear, is...' Her heart did a crazy somer-
sault at that 'my dear', and she stared at him,
for this time *his* voice seemed to have died on
him. Manfully, however, he resuscitated it, and
went on, his grey eyes holding hers, 'The big
deal, Jazzlyn, is that I—care about you.'

She stared numbly at him—then hastily she
looked away, so he should glean nothing of the
riot of emotions that were in uproar within her
at his words. Care? What did 'care' mean?
Care—I'll look out for you? Care—because
we're friends? Or care—because... Jazzlyn
couldn't finish that one.

'You're—attracted to me. You said so
once,' she remembered when she had found
any sort of a voice. Caring, attraction—were
they one and the same thing? Her brain, her
thinking powers, seemed to have deserted her.

'I've been attracted to you from the very
beginning,' Holden stated—and Jazzlyn, even
while knowing that his eyes were on her, just
had to swallow.

But a girl still had her pride. 'Go on—surprise me!' she invited, endeavouring to sound
cool, only to go and spoil it when she just had
to recap. 'From the very beginning, you said?'

'From the first time I saw you,' he confirmed.

'When you came to my home?' Her brain didn't seem to be working on all cylinders; she needed to absorb this very slowly and very carefully. If, for some reason best known to himself, Holden was leading her some merry dance around the sand dunes, then she wanted to be able to spot it and stop him when he put a foot wrong.

'From that very first time I came to your home,' he confirmed. 'You opened the door and for the first time in my life I was struck speechless.'

Solemnly Jazzlyn stared at him. 'By—me?' she asked.

'By you—your beauty.'

Her eyes went wide. 'You must know dozens of beautiful women.'

'But none that make my heart give a thump as it did when you opened the door to me that day,' he stated—and Jazzlyn's head went floating high in the clouds for several unbelievable seconds.

'You—er—told my father you'd come to enquire about Grace's birthday dinner,'

Jazzlyn commented, striving quite desperately to keep her feet firmly planted on the ground.

'Jazzlyn, I want only to be honest with you, and I do ask your forgiveness that I lied when I told your father that I'd called since I was passing that way.'

'You came purposely to check him out,' she stated coldly, the chill voice of reality hooting at any nonsensical idea that Holden might have come to care for her in the way she so desperately wanted him to care for her.

'I did, and—' He broke off. 'Hell,' he muttered, 'I knew this wasn't going to be easy— and I haven't got started yet!'

'I can easily leave!' Jazzlyn retorted.

'No way!' he answered before she could blink. 'I'm never going to have this kind of opportunity again.'

'No one around and me a *captive* audience!' she tossed back sniffily. 'Make the most of it!'

'I thoroughly intend to. I've suffered enough, held back too much, to want to let this moment go!'

'You've suffered...' Held back! Her brain seemed to have gone addled again. 'You were saying?' she prompted—perhaps if he went

back a step she might find some sort of com-
prehension.

To her surprise, Holden switched back to
what he had been saying—as if it was important to him to get all past dishonesties cleared
so that he might move on. 'I was saying,' he
resumed, 'that I called at your home purposely.
I'd started to grow concerned myself, even
without my mother phoning. Bearing in mind
my aunt's gullibility—she'd spent years believing Archie Craddock's lies—when my
mother asked if I'd call and check out this
three times married Edwin Palmer her sister
was seeing so much of I was only too glad to.'

Jazzlyn had known since the night of his
aunt's birthday dinner that Holden had been
checking to see what sort of man her father
was, but even so she tried to get angry at
Holden's nerve. Had she not met and grown
fond of Grace she might have succeeded. But
Grace had such a sweetness of nature—she
laid herself wide open to being taken advantage of. Jazzlyn, therefore, felt it seemed trite
to express the sarcastic hope that her father had
checked out well. But she couldn't help but
feel that some challenge was needed.

'I wonder you could bear to invite him to be your guest at dinner!' she offered tartly—and was in for another surprise when Holden seemed to accept her waspish tone as his due.

He didn't take her up on it, anyhow, but confessed, 'I'd no such intention when I rang your doorbell. Then I saw you—and within minutes of meeting your father I'm suggesting that the four of us celebrate my aunt's birthday together.'

'I thought to include me was an after-thought!' It slipped out before Jazzlyn knew it.

'My dear,' Holden said softly, 'you were my first thought.'

Her brain scrambled again. The cold front she was striving so hard to establish at once vanished into thin air. 'Don't, Holden!' she cried, that 'my dear' enough without the rest of it.

His answer was to move swiftly from the chair he had been sitting on to come and join her on the sofa. 'Don't be upset,' he soothed, taking hold of one of her hands in his. 'I prom-ise, I'm trying only to—to make things right. You're the last person I would ever want to harm.'

She drew a shaky breath. 'Let me go, then!' she begged, such a trembling going on inside her to have him gently holding her hand that she knew herself in grave danger of revealing that she was indeed in love with him.

'I—can't,' Holden refused.

'You can't?'

'Have I hidden my feelings so well you have no idea what you mean to me?'

Oh, Holden! Was caring—simply caring? Or—that giant question—was caring—love? It was a question she couldn't ask. Was afraid to ask. Because it couldn't be, could it?

'I—er—didn't know you had any—feelings for me—particularly,' she murmured as airily as she was able.

His answer was to lean towards her and to lightly touch his lips to hers. Unblinking, un-moving, she sat stunned and stared at him. 'Sweet Jazzlyn, I don't suppose you did,' he said softly. 'But believe me when I tell you I've been swamped with all sorts of feelings and emotions over you.'

She didn't believe it—yet he'd said he wanted only to be honest with her. Surely he couldn't have been hammered by the kind of emotions she'd been through over him? 'Such as?' She found she could no more hold back from asking than fly.

And Holden did not hold back from accepting her invitation. 'Where to start? Raging jealousy! Sl—'

'Raging jealousy?' she asked in a rush. 'When were you ever jealous?'

'How long have you got?' he replied with a gentle smile. 'Rex Alford kissing your cheek, flirting with you…'

'You were jealous of Rex?' she exclaimed, thoroughly startled.

'Furiously jealous,' Holden admitted openly.

'But—but we barely knew each other—you and I!' she gasped.

'Don't I know it! It was crazy, this emotion that roared through me to see you laughing with some other man. This enchantment, this thumping in my heart region during the rest of my aunt's celebratory dinner.'

Jazzlyn stared at him, mesmerised. 'You were—enchanted? By—m-me!' she whispered, utterly staggered.

'My dear,' he said softly, gently, 'it was a shaker to me too. This feeling that coursed through me for you was such a totally new experience to me, it caught me out of my depth—had me floundering.'

'I'd...' Her throat was dry, and she had to swallow again before she could continue. 'I'd no idea!' she exclaimed chokily. She looked into his eyes and her heartbeats, which for the past few minutes had been going into over-drive, started to race some more. She saw only sincerity in his grey glance. A look there that said, Believe me, trust me.

'How could you have any idea?' he asked. 'I was fighting like the devil to hide it. And, my darling,' he went on, 'I've been at the greatest of pains ever since to hide how com-pletely bowled over by you I was—and am.'

She coughed, nerves attacking. Caring, bowled over—love? Still she couldn't ask— was suddenly too terrified to ask, in case the great joy that was trying to burst out within her did get free—but all for nothing.

'You managed it magnificently,' she whis-pered.

Tenderly, Holden kissed her lips again. 'Sweet Jazzlyn, I had to take myself off home that night to try and sort myself out.'

'Did—you manage it?'

'Hardly. My head was in a spin. I wanted to see you again—but we'd just had a small quarrel in that car park. Also, you were pretty cagey about relationships.'

'I'm not!' she denied.

'How many men have you dated more than three times?' he countered.

He had her there. But…! 'You wanted to see me more than three times?' she asked in a rush, her eyes going huge as what she thought he was trying to convey started to register.

'Oh, yes, many more times than that,' he owned. 'Did I not say I was enchanted by you?'

'Oh, Holden,' Jazzlyn murmured tremulously.

'Don't be afraid, little love,' he breathed. 'I'll never harm you.'

The only thing she was afraid of just then was of being so confused that she was reading this all wrong. It was all too brilliantly wonderful if Holden truly did care for her in the loving way she so wanted. But even while she was starting to trust what his eyes, his gentleness were telling her, it was herself, her instincts, which were crying, Yes, oh, yes, that—because it was so wonderful—she was afraid to trust.

'You—um—left it a week before you got in touch with me again,' she thought to mention, from that part of her brain that was still functioning. 'And then only because some avaricious female was after you.'

'Lies, all lies,' Holden owned, and then, while Jazzlyn stared at him, puzzled, 'Had there been any such woman I'd have been quite able to handle the situation without help.' He smiled.

'You're saying that there was no such…?'

'I'll never lie to you again,' he promised, and Jazzlyn blinked at that, because surely to make such a promise—and in that way—it must mean that even if he did not want an affair with her—and she owned she was extremely confused about that and a good deal else—it must mean that he wanted them to be friends in future, for them to see each other again! 'But,' he went on, 'to lie seemed a necessary evil at the time.'

She looked at him, unable to sort out any answer, 'Why?' she just had to ask.

'Because—' he began, but then—again giving her the oddest impression that he was a little nervous of the ground he was on—he broke off. Stretching out to take both her hands in his, he explained, 'I wanted to get close to you, Jazzlyn. I wanted us to get to know each other. But what chance would I have when— if I was lucky and you actually agreed to go out with me—it would be three dates only, then, Bye-bye, Holden?'

Her eyes shot saucer-wide. 'Good heavens!' she gasped, amazed at the way his thoughts had gone.

'I know,' he agreed. 'I was fairly staggered myself that I could be so devious—but then I'd never been in love before. So, if you went out with me purely as protection against some money-minded—' He broke off. 'What's the matter?' he asked urgently. 'You look stunned. I only thought that, if you agreed, it wouldn't count as a date as such, but…'

'Wh-what did you say?' she asked huskily.

'About my lie and—?'

'B-before that,' she interrupted chokily. 'You—um—said something about never having been in—love, before—er…'

'I did, but—' He broke off again. 'See where you've got me, woman?' he growled. 'I don't know where I'm at! I thought I'd been telling you all this while of my caring, my love for you.' His love! For her! Unspeaking, tremulous, she solemnly stared at him. 'Oh, dear, dear, dearest Jazzlyn, I think the whole world of you,' he revealed ardently. 'I love you, my sweet darling. I'm so much in love with you I've been half off my head with it!'

'Oh, Holden,' she whispered.

He kissed her. 'You do love me, don't you?' he asked. 'You weren't lying when you said that you did?' he demanded urgently.

'I wasn't lying,' she confirmed shyly.

Holden looked very much as if he would kiss her again. Though first he appeared to have a more pressing need. 'You wouldn't care to repeat it, I suppose?' he asked, and, incredibly, Jazzlyn discerned a look of strain in his eyes.

She smiled at him—how dear he was to her. 'I love you,' she said, 'Oh, Holden Hathaway, I do so love you.'

'Jazzlyn!' he cried, and a moment later she was in his arms, being held close up against his heart 'Jazzlyn, Jazzlyn,' he crooned, and kissed her brow, and held her, and looked into her eyes. 'You're sure?'

'I'm positive. You?'

'Indelible in my heart from almost that first moment. When?' he asked.

'Did I know I was in love with you?'

'Please?' he answered.

'That night—last Monday—when you—er—after you'd fixed my TV set.'

'Oh, lovely Jazzlyn. Then—that wonderful night! Oh, how I wanted to stay with you that night!'

'You went—left me,' she reproached him lovingly.

'I had to,' he replied, and explained, 'I loved you so much, wanted you so much—you were responsive—and yet I feared I was treading on very fragile ground.'

'Because you didn't know that I loved you?'

'Because, my darling…' he began, but hesitated a good while before, as if making up his mind about something, he proceeded, 'Because, Jazzlyn, while I love and desire you with everything that's in me, I want more from you than that we become lovers.'

She stared at him. Her mouth went dry again. 'You t-told me once that you didn't want an affair,' she reminded him.

'I do not,' he stated firmly. 'Neither do I want just three dates with you and to be told, No more. Yet, at the same time, I'm half terrified to tell you what it is that I *do* want, in case you're not ready to trust and I scare you off for ever.'

Once more she stared at him. 'You're talking in riddles again,' she managed, feeling confused, her brain seeking, but a poor thing when it came to deciphering what it was that Holden did want.

'Blame yourself, little Jazzlyn.' He smiled. 'Before I met you I had a well-ordered life and was an honest, upstanding member of the community.'

'I changed all that?' she exclaimed.

'Prior to knowing you, I would never have thought of deviously inviting my aunt to come and spend a holiday here.'

Taken aback, Jazzlyn pulled away to look at him. 'Grace has holidayed here at Sandbanks before,' she stated, puzzled.

'True,' he agreed. 'Only this time it was different. Aunt Grace had told me how concerned she was that Tony Johnstone's pestering was getting you down, and how she'd suggested to you that you went away for a while. On my part, I'd been planning how best I could next see you. It then seemed to me little short of brilliant that I should suggest to her that *she* looked as though she could do with a break and invite her and your father to take a breath of sea air at my home for a few weeks.'

'You thought Grace would invite me?'

'I was sure she would. Just as I knew she would be in touch to ask if I'd mind.'

'Good heavens!' Jazzlyn gasped, stunned. 'You didn't mind? You wanted me here?'

'My darling, if I could get you to Sandbanks I would take some time off work, see you every day—no need to ask you out. We could get to know each other. Perhaps you'd learn to trust me. Perhaps we could go on from there—' he broke off. 'I do so love you,' he told her tenderly.

'Oh, Holden!' she cried, and, like a homing pigeon, she went closer to him, and for long minutes they held each other in wonder and love. 'Grace didn't tell me that I was holidaying in your home,' Jazzlyn murmured, joy breaking over her like waves to be in his arms, to feel his tender kisses on her face. 'Did you ask her not to?'

'My aunt, as you probably know, hasn't a devious bone in her body. I knew her main concern was to get you away from Tony Johnstone and more relaxed than you were. I hoped to be here before you found out. Though it's true—' he smiled '—that I did suggest to her that you'd probably relax more if the name of your host was unknown to you for a few days.'

'Grace agreed?'

'She said she'd do her best but that she wasn't telling lies. And that she'd have to tell your father. But she added that at times he was so lovably vague it might not fully register.'

'You're quite a rogue, aren't you?' Jazzlyn exclaimed, faintly astonished at the way he had worked things out.

'I'm a man in love, my darling. A man quite desperately in love, and I needed some time with you. As I said—to get you here at Sandbanks was quite a brilliant notion.'

Jazzlyn felt all misty-eyed. 'I do love you!' she sighed—and as Holden looked adoringly down at her it seemed the most natural thing in the world that they should hold each other close, should kiss and hold, and kiss again, this time lingeringly. 'Oh,' Jazzlyn breathed as their kiss ended.

'You don't know where you are either?' Holden suggested softly.

'Floating!' she smiled.

'I adore you.'

They kissed again, and as that wonderful kiss ended Jazzlyn just had to tell him, 'I'm so glad you came back today.'

'No more than I, my darling,' he breathed. 'I didn't want to leave. In fact, how I managed to tear myself away from you on Tuesday I shall never know.'

'You kissed me goodbye,' she murmured dreamily. 'A wonderful, gentle kiss of good-bye. But—' she smiled '—duty called. You had work to do.'

'Sweet love. I didn't leave on Tuesday because my work called.'

'You didn't?' she asked, surprised.

'My dear, we'd kissed. The previous evening, when I'd come into your room to fiddle with your television set. We'd kissed, and by that time I was aching with my love for you. I needed just a little solace. But one kiss, I found, wasn't enough. I was parched for your tenderness, your arms. I wanted more.'

'Oh, my darling!' she cried. He sounded like a soul in torment. Jazzlyn kissed him, purely because she just had to.

'If you do that much more I shall forget what we were saying.' He smiled tenderly.

'We were saying... *You* were saying,' she corrected, and had to own she was feeling more than a little woolly-headed herself. 'That—um—if I remember rightly—that you didn't leave here on Tuesday because work called.'

'You're smart.' He kissed her. 'It wasn't a case of work calling, my love, but sanity calling.'

'Sanity?' She was intrigued.

'We'd kissed, you and I. Oh, how we'd kissed!' he inserted with a smile, and seemed to love her sudden bashful look, and kissed her nose. 'And I quite desperately wanted to go on making love to you, to make you mine,' he added softly.

'W-why didn't you?' she asked shyly, going a little pink about the ears.

'My honest love.' He smiled. 'I adore you even more, if possible, for not pretending.' Jazzlyn smiled back at him, realising that he'd known full well that she'd have made no demur had he carried on to make her his that night. He kissed her tenderly once more, and then took up, 'I wanted you—oh, so much. Yet I had to tear myself away. Take myself off. Cool down. Clear my head. I wanted you so much I couldn't think. But instinct was telling me that it was all wrong.' He kissed her bewildered face. 'I wanted more than to make complete love with you, my darling. You'd said that you liked me more than any man you know—and I wanted more than that too.'

'You wanted my love?'

'I wanted you,' he said, and held her very firmly to him as he added, his eyes steady on hers, 'I want you permanently in my life, Jazzlyn.'

She jumped, jerked away, her eyes huge in her face. Holden held her steady. She swallowed. 'You do?' she asked shakily, a kind of roaring going on in her ears.

'I do,' he said firmly, and Jazzlyn had never seen him so serious or so rock-solid. 'I was never more certain about anything than I am about that. I went away on Tuesday because I felt if I gave in to this desperate desire I have for you I stood to ruin any small chance I had with you. I was awake all that Monday night, wanting you—you sleeping nearby—responsive. I'd said I wasn't thinking straight and neither was I—I needed to get away to try and think clearly.'

'Did you think clearly—when you were away, I mean? You said, when you went on Tuesday, that—um—though you were attracted to me...'

'*Very* attracted,' he interrupted, to show he had forgotten not a word of what he'd said.

'Very attracted,' she resumed. 'But you didn't want an affair with me.' She swallowed. 'Have you—changed your mind?'

Deliberately, slowly, he shook his head. 'I have not,' he replied steadfastly.

'Oh!' she mumbled. 'Er—you want us to be good friends?'

'With my arms around you like this? Good friends—and more.' He smiled.

'I'm foxed!' she admitted.

'And I'm terrified of scaring you off,' Holden stated.

Jazzlyn stared at him. 'Wh…? You're terrified of—' She broke off. 'I don't understand,' she confessed, her confusion complete.

'I love you, Jazzlyn. I have from the first. I drove home that night after my aunt's birthday dinner knowing, despite our small quarrel, that I was utterly enchanted by you. I knew then what I wanted.' He broke off to give her shoulders a small squeeze. 'But how to gain my heart's desire? I resorted to lying.'

Jazzlyn pushed through some of her confusion to remark, fairly coherently, she thought, 'You—decided to invite me to a dinner...'

'Where some woman was supposed to be after my wallet,' he took up. 'Lies, all lies. I loved you, my darling, and wanted your love, yet felt I couldn't let you know by word or look this torrent of feeling in me for you. For my sins, I found it irksome in the extreme to have to consign myself to patience while falling deeper and deeper in love with you all the while.'

'Has it been so very irksome—loving me?' she asked, still feeling slightly astonished that Holden had loved her all this while!

'You've no idea,' he said softly. 'I danced only once with you at that dinner. Just holding you in my arms I was losing control. I didn't dare dance with you again.'

'Oh!' she sighed.

'You might say, ''Oh'',' he teased. 'There am I, holding back from coming down here when you arrived the other Saturday for fear of rushing things—only to find when I get here that you've already made a date with someone else.'

'Who? Oh. David Musgrove. Er—if it makes you feel any better, I'll confess I was very happy that Monday—happy that you were here.'

'Keep telling me things like that, my darling. I truly need to hear them.'

'Honestly?'

'Only ever honest from now on,' he promised. He kissed her deeply then, and very satisfyingly, but pulled back to confess, 'You've no idea of the times I've had to put a tight rein on my feelings.'

'I'd like to hear, if I may,' she encouraged with a light laugh.

'There were so many times when I've ached, just ached to hold you in my arms. We swam—in clothes, we swam once—and I loved you. I've suffered hell with jealousy, yet somehow—purely because I wasn't going to have Musgrove kissing you goodnight—I stayed around when he brought you home from your date.'

'Killjoy—you had a date yourself that night,' she reminded him.

'I didn't—but I wasn't averse to you thinking I had,' he confessed.

'You...' she gasped. Then, 'Rotter!' she be-called him lovingly. 'If I'm honest...'

'I insist on only honesty between us from now on,' Holden put in.

'Then I'll own to wanting to ask who your date had been. Only I couldn't. I suppose I must have been jealous without fully realising it.'

'Music—sweet music to me,' Holden grinned, admitting, 'It was music, too, to hear you state as we drove to the supermarket that you'd probably miss me when I returned to London. Did you?' he blatantly fished.

'You were in my head the whole time,' she admitted, then felt his warm hug to her shoulders and added, 'I knew by then that I loved you so much. I was feeling quite desolate—and it wasn't helped when some woman I didn't take to at all rang to speak to you yesterday. That was when I really knew what jealousy—stomach-churning, relentless jealousy—truly felt like.'

Holden kissed her for her pain, but owned, 'Forgive me, my love, but I seem to be highly attuned to you, and I sensed a hint of jealousy there when I phoned and you said you'd told my caller that you were my live-in girlfriend.'

'Did you mind?'

'*Mind!* I was electrified. Ye gods, that had to be jealousy in your voice! Only the merest hint, I grant. But—dare I believe it? And what in thunder am I doing in London when you're down here? Darling, darling Jazzlyn, I knew then only that I must see you with all speed.'

'But you left it until today?'

'Nerves set in,' he admitted. 'But after another sleepless night—you've got a nerve telling me I look tired,' he inserted. 'I never knew what insomnia was until I met you.' She beamed in delight and, encouraged, he kissed her again and went on. 'But, my own darling, I got here, and after weeks—agonising weeks, I might add—of holding back, of knowing I risked what I ultimately wanted to achieve should I give in to the ever-present urge to kiss you, to hold you, to tell you how your smile lights up my life, I think the time is right to—' He broke off, and to Jazzlyn's mind he seemed to be under some kind of strain again.

'Is right to…?' she just had to prompt, to try and help—simply, she loved him.

Holden took a steadying breath. 'It won't do!' he declared. 'I've been skirting around the issue for long enough—have come close a couple of times, but got cold feet in case this was where it all went horrendously wrong. I told myself you needed some kind of explanation for my actions—when basically, after you seemed to jerkily take fright, I got scared and backed off. But—enough,' he said firmly.

Jazzlyn swallowed. She had no idea of what was coming, but that look of strain was still there and she wanted to help him—but he looked so serious. 'What?' was the best she could manage that time.

'I now know that you return my love,' he said. 'I felt, last Saturday, without knowing if it was a good sign or bad, that my nearness to you as our hands met at the kitchen sink was disturbing you in some way.'

'It was,' she agreed. She thought he might smile, but he did not, and his expression remained the same—set, strained, yet strangely resolute—as he went on.

'Jazzlyn, my dear, you said—that Saturday, in that supermarket,' he reminded her, and it seemed then as if he had never forgotten a

word of everything she had ever told him
'—that you had never met a man whom you
would wish to be the father of your child.'

Her eyes shot wide and she stared at him.
'I—remember,' she agreed, and at the intense
look in his eyes—not to mention the fact that
the arm about her shoulders was suddenly
holding her very, very firmly—she swallowed
hard.

'Then, I wonder how you feel—that is—if
you love me well enough, my adorable
Jazzlyn, to be the mother of my children?'

Her breath caught, and, while her heart positively thundered as it banged against her ribs,
she feared she might faint. She licked suddenly
dry lips. 'You—want to—p-play house?' she
questioned huskily.

Holden shook his head. 'My dear, I want
more than that.'

Her brain seized up. 'Oh!' she managed.

'What I want,' he stated, his eyes steady on
her face, 'is a tidy certificate to precede our
children.'

'Oh!' she gasped again. 'You mean a...'
She couldn't finish.

'I mean a marriage certificate,' Holden finished for her, holding her firmly when she instinctively went to move away. 'Don't be alarmed, my darling,' he soothed. 'I know that where I've had marriage in mind from the beginning I haven't given you any time at all to adjust to the idea, but...'

'You've—had m-marriage in mind from the beginning?' she echoed croakily.

'I have,' he agreed, confessing, 'Initially, before we met, it was my aunt I was concerned about. But when you and I met everything else soon became secondary—and I became more concerned about you.'

'Me? Why?'

'Because—for all I deliberately told you how I felt I could relax with you, because I knew you wouldn't be plotting to get me to the altar—to get you to the altar is exactly what I've been plotting to do all this while.'

Jazzlyn stared at him in amazement, her heartbeats still going nineteen to the dozen. 'Truly!' She couldn't believe it—any of it. Holden was proposing marriage! Correction—*had* proposed!

'Truly,' he confirmed. 'I haven't been open with you before because I knew I would have had you running scared if you'd any idea of what was in my head and heart. But all that must end now. I came here this morning—and nearly had heart failure, incidentally, when I found the house locked up and thought you'd gone.'

'You—I was walking on the beach,' she stated unnecessarily—Holden had come to meet her, so he already knew that. But some kind of inner freedom was exploding within her, and she was having a hard time concentrating on anything—save that Holden had proposed!

'I came looking for you after a sprint up to your bedroom showed your suitcase was still here.'

'I—thought you'd come in person to tell me to leave,' she confessed huskily.

'Never that, my darling. I want you to live here with me, and be with me wherever I am. Don't you know yet? Haven't you realised that, wanting so to see you, I was struck dumb this morning and just wanted to feast my eyes on your enchanting face?'

'Oh—H-Holden!' she cried, her voice starting to go all wobbly.

'Oh, my darling, trust me!' he implored. 'Let me help you overcome the one drawback I referred to—your hang-up about marriage. Together we can wipe out all past traumas. I love you. You love me. Jazzlyn, oh, Jazzlyn, together we can tackle anything. I promise.'

Jazzlyn looked at him for long, long moments. She saw the love he held for her there in his eyes, and at last she gave a shaky sigh. 'Oh, Holden,' she whispered. 'It was only yesterday that I decided, most definitely, that I was never going to marry.'

Holden blanched. But he wasn't taking that. 'And today?' he questioned toughly. 'What about today, Jazzlyn, now that you know you hold my heart, my life, in your hands?'

She smiled, and told him quickly, 'Today I believe I will—but only if the right man asks me.'

'Sweet love,' Holden breathed, with no let-up in his tense expression. 'Am I the right man?'

'You know you are,' she whispered.

'My love,' he cried, and, cradling her, he kissed her. '*Will* you marry me?' he urged intensely.

'I—er—don't think I'd find the strains of the ''Wedding March'' too jarring after all.' She smiled.

'My darling!' Her 'yes' was in her eyes, in her smile, and in her choice of music to be played in church. But still he wanted more confirmation. 'Is that a yes?' he demanded throatily.

'It's a yes. A definite, most definite yes,' she replied huskily.

'Oh—I do love you!' he cried exultantly. One kiss was not enough.